Negativeland

Doug Nufer

Autonomedia

Parts of *Negativeland* were slightly altered to appear
in *Word Ways* magazine and in the anthology
Help Yourself! (Autonomedia).

Acknowledgments:
I cannot give enough thanks to Harry Mathews, Michael
Upchurch, Rebecca Brown, Gilbert Sorrentino, my editors
Ron Kolm and Jim Feast of the Unbearables, Jim Fleming,
Masae Sato, and Ben Meyers of Autonomedia, my former
agent Susan Schorr, and my first reader Kathleen Skeels.

 This publication is made possible in part with
public funds from the New York State Council
on the Arts, a state agency.

NYSCA

Cover Art: David Lasky
Author Photo: Casey Kelbaugh
Iconography: Russell Christian
Print Design: Masae Sato

Autonomedia
POB 568 Williamsburgh Station
Brooklyn, New York 11211-0568 USA

Email: info@autonomedia.org
Website: www.autonomedia.org

Printed in Canada

For El, Ed, and Bessie

Negativeland has nothing to do
with the band Negativland.

No characters or scenes in *Negativeland* come from life.

And, for the record, the winner of the
men's 100-meter and 200-meter backstroke events
in the 1972 Olympics was not an American,
but Roland Matthes of East Germany.

Nobody gets to live life backwards.
                                        —Ann Landers

-6

None of the stations played anything good, but I kept at the buttons, pushing off songs from a childhood we were all supposed to have had. Commercials bothered me more than ever, news was propaganda, and traffic reports were no more useful than the weather. It wasn't yet 1988, and I was driving home from Tacoma.

I liked Tacoma because it wasn't Seattle, the same as I liked Seattle because it wasn't New York, and vice-versa.

Radio was better before, when Larry King didn't interview so many movie stars and the college stations made a stab at doing what nobody else would do, but tapes were for dentists, records were for garage sales, and CDs were the rich stealing from the poor. I stuck with radio because you never knew.

On came a voice anyone from that childhood could-n't help knowing, just him and an electric guitar before a live audience. Even live, the dead song stunned me, and the audience kept quiet until — on cue and not off key — they hummed the organ part.

"Don't you remember," she said, "how we used to split exacts, the time we almost hit the pick six; speed figures, trip notes, speed, trips . . . don't you remember the track?"

"I don't remember lots of things."

"Come on, Chick, don't be like that."

"I'll tell you what I don't remember."

"No Chick, please, I'll do anything you say."

"No you won't."

Miriam never wore what I wanted her to wear, as if what I would have said should have mattered. She didn't even put her lipstick on right, laying it on thick in reds the shop clerks told her were for black women, even though she was white enough to sell her veins. She was one of the last people I knew who wasn't afraid to smoke and drink. She wasn't any older than I was; she was my landlady and I was her friend.

"Take me to the dogs, Chick, it's not too late. Turn the car around and we'll go to Portland and live like Monday never comes. No kidding, what have we got to lose? If not the dogs, maybe the Beavers, or we'll drive to the beach through the wine country. Come on, baby, why the hell not?"

"You don't want to know."

"Don't, Chick — be nice."

We never did anything, so I wanted to make her birthday a surprise. That wouldn't be hard.

She worked in a photo lab developing negatives and I was unemployed. They didn't hire people who had spent more than a year working for nobody else and for five years I'd worked for myself. When the city got into the recycling business, you couldn't sell trash for chickenfeed. Miriam said it was a blessing in disguise, that you shouldn't spend the rest of your life going through garbage, but she couldn't deny there were worse jobs because she hated her own.

Minor league baseball was cheaper than the track, but these Sunday games left us with little to look forward to beyond another week of hated work and dreaded unemployment. This always bothered me a little, and when the old song came on the radio it bothered me a lot, like it wasn't just an old song on the radio.

But then, I couldn't have been alone in not wanting to think about when I was young.

"Know why you're not an asshole, Chick? You don't pass judgment. I could tell you I married for money, that I poisoned the old man eight different ways before I finally managed to kill him, and you'd say, 'We've all made mistakes.'"

I never told Miriam how I liked the way she called me not by my first name, but by the last syllable of my last name.

"He had to take me out every night because if he didn't, I would go alone."

And I never told her how I didn't like the way she talked about Boyd because in a way, I did.

"You know what they say about guys like that," she said, "not with a bang but a whimper."

We were in the Mirror Lounge, about the only place where she hadn't pulled her trick of passing notes to busboys. Once Boyd intercepted a note, one that said what the others said: I don't want you; I'm just doing this to make him jealous. Not, my husband: him.

Boyd couldn't get to his lawyer fast enough.

"Never marry for love, never fuck for money, and never lie," she said, winking.

Boyd couldn't have loved her and he only pretended that he didn't care. He tried to brag about her by saying that he, of all men, had her in a way that nobody else had. He told me things he shouldn't have. With nothing better to do, I listened.

A heart attack in a fifty-year-old fat man with bad habits was no cause for autopsy. In the end, Miriam should have been flattered that he mortgaged his buildings and unloaded his stock in order to keep up with her. She wasn't.

"Never lie for money, never fuck for marriage, and never love."

You couldn't tell her she hadn't earned her share. It wasn't just a marriage: it was nine months of her life! The medical school took Boyd and the banks got the rest, except for one crummy building even a full time job couldn't maintain. Rents might have paid the bills, but Miriam never had made the adjustment from tenant to landlady. Not that she was soft; she only believed that people had a right to fair rent. Like most of her ideas, Miriam's notion of fair rent came from a time that never was.

"Never love for money, never fuck for lying, and never marry."

When she found how little was left of his estate, Miriam didn't hide her contempt. Could she sue a dead man for not leaving her all he had after he had spent the rest trying to make sure that she wouldn't be miserable? Two years ago that was, and still she joked about how many fat men she'd have to go through so she wouldn't die broke, which made her wonder how the student doctors ever got through to Boyd. When she said they probably had to borrow a chainsaw from the School of Forestry, she didn't have to go on.

She couldn't sell the building any more than she could evict the deadbeats. The offers weren't good enough and every one came from developers who want-

ed to tear it down. Ours wasn't a bad neighborhood —
in a bad way, it was good. Nobody living in Miriam's
building could afford to shop in the nearby stores, so the
solution was to get rid of the apartments and put in
parking lots to give people who could afford to shop
places for their cars.

"Never marry, never lie. Never love, never fuck."

Money went without saying. The graph of life went
from upper left to lower right and you didn't have to ask
Y to know the answer would be X, the known unknown.

We weren't much for philosophy, and history was a
sore subject, especially on Miriam's birthday in an
empty cocktail lounge. The Mirror had no other customers because it was closed: my surprise present to
Miriam. The owner didn't mind. He knew we were
harmless and that we'd pass out before we drank what
I had paid for the use of his booze. He knew we would-
n't eat the nuts or drink anything but martinis, but he
was wrong. Because it was a special night, we drank
Johnny Walker, and not the red label, either.

It should have been more special, but Miriam was
disappointed, as if we really could have gone to
Portland, the wine country, and the coast. Renting a bar
for a private party wasn't unexpected, even if she could-
n't deny it was a treat and it might have been a surprise.

She drank off her lipstick and put it back on, I undid
my tie.

"Bet you can't guess what I really want," she said, "a
trip to Hawaii."

"Don't expect me to take you."

"No shit."

"You wouldn't want a pineapple upside down shake
instead?"

"No way."

"You only want what you can't have."

Even with the lights off, the Mirror wasn't dark. Street glare wouldn't leave a room where every wall was glass. It wasn't small, but seemed larger. We were no more than two, but seemed multiplied, squared and cubed. Nothing was as it should have been, reversed. Maybe it hadn't been such a good idea for the owner to leave us unattended in a room full of mirrors and alcohol. Clarity disrupted us. We couldn't tell the difference between space and wall. In a place built for reflection the problem was that, without warning, you might somehow pass through to another way of coming back to where you supposed you were.

"Forget about Hawaii," I said, forgetting that I wasn't talking to myself.

"I don't get it. Ohhhh, but you've been there, haven't you?"

"Who hasn't?"

"I haven't and I want to go."

"No you don't. It wasn't anything like you think. It wasn't paradise."

"Paradise schmaradise — wasn't it fun?"

"It wasn't awful."

With opposing mirrors reversing each other toward infinity, I saw I couldn't avoid going back over Hawaii. Miriam wanted to know, but I had to know, because it hadn't always been like this, because somewhere back there, things went wrong.

As the road west led east, I couldn't go forward without looking back, beginning at the end.

I left Hawaii without a tan but with some kind of disease. Going to the doctor for a cold would have been pointless and not until it went away months later did somebody tell me it was something curable by drugs. I

wanted nothing more to do with drugs. There was no
excuse for it, but drugs were the reason for my trip. This
wasn't long after my divorce. Nobody could blame me
for wanting to make a little money on a business trip
that could pass for a vacation, even if it meant going
along as Wolfie's pack mule.

We stayed on the Big Island with friends, although
they weren't my friends as much as Wolfie's: Frank
and Linda. Frank sold real estate in one of those no-
money-down schemes advertised in half-hour commercials that mimicked legitimate TV shows, and yet
Wolfie didn't believe Frank when Frank said he had
quit growing marijuana. Eventually, even Wolfie
understood that this wasn't going to be an expenses-
paid junket but an expensive vacation.

Not that Wolfie minded. The kids getting sick, the
parents fighting, the bad TV reception, the greasy food,
the steady rain, the muggy sun, and the fact that the trip
was a total loss couldn't help giving him a sense of
accomplishment. Best of all, we were no more than a
few hundred yards away from the ocean, but couldn't
go in the water.

We borrowed the truck with the expired inspection
sticker and drove around looking for a place where you
could get through the coral without losing your skin.
We couldn't stop until we toured the whole island
because there was too much to see, but then a storm hit.
Dozens of eucalyptus trees fell across the main road,
killing power so the pumps wouldn't work. We ran out
of gas, but not before a wave broke over the car on the
strip of the big town on the Kona coast.

Wolfie couldn't wait to tell Frank, but he really
wanted to impress Linda. Big and shaggy, Wolfie went
for women who were small and trim, and for a woman
to want to have nothing to do with him wasn't enough.

She had to be unattainable.

I tried not to notice them by playing with the kids. The one-year-old was stuck in a perpetual motion swing that clicked like a clock so she wouldn't cry. We had a game where I'd give her a ball, she'd throw it, I'd retrieve and she'd throw it again — not much of a game, but it beat playing with her brother. Her brother had been kicked out of daycare for fighting, so he watched dinosaur videos and went around whacking me with a plastic sword that wasn't supposed to hurt.

None of this was supposed to matter, even though Wolfie meant it when he asked Frank how much he wanted for his wife.

"Not for the week, just the night."

"Nope — you take her, she's yours, plus kids."

"Twenty minutes," said Wolfie, "no more."

"Twenty minutes, twenty years," said Frank, "makes no difference."

Conversation was no more than a dialogue that ended in arm wrestling. Wolfie wanted to wrestle Viking Style, with a fire going on each side of the table, but Frank didn't want to burn the house down... yet.

He'd bought it for nothing and was going to sell it as soon as he painted over the scum. It wasn't a house so much as a fiberglass octagon with a tin roof on a foundation of stilts. Even treated for termites, it couldn't go a year without a complete fumigation, the only time it was safe from thieves.

Linda had refused to move in and threatened to take the kids to California, but after a night in a Hilo motel she saw it was hopeless to resist. Besides, they had to be here so their stuff wouldn't get stolen.

"Sometimes we miss the shotgun," said Linda, but she didn't miss the way things had been. Three houses before this one, thieves took the shotgun along with half of Frank's marijuana crop, so he couldn't go to the cops because the rest of the crop was still there. Defenseless, they finally gave up when other growers planted mines in the fields. Yet there was no way to persuade Miriam that Frank and Linda should have left Hawaii for Texas in July.

"It was the hottest summer anyone could remember," said Linda, dreamy-eyed, as if she wasn't talking to me but narrating a movie. "I'd eat a pill and hours later it would be just as hot and I'd eat another pill because nothing changed. I'd come to over the sink, the water running down my wrists, hundreds — no, thousands — of precious gallons wasted. What was I doing there and not where I'd been? Weren't we going to do something with soybeans or goats? There was nothing to eat, so we ate rattlesnakes, but Frank couldn't kill them on downers, so we went back to Mexico for speed.

"First he shot them, only that didn't work because they'd get riddled or blown to bits. It took a while before he wasn't scared of using the noose gizmo. Even with boots, you can't be too sure of the strike."

Linda the valium pioneer looked back at that summer in Texas from a winter in a house she hated and I couldn't help wanting to take her with me. As Frank and Wolfie went from gas station to gas station trying to get an updated inspection sticker, Linda and I sipped rum in hammocks under palms, looking at an unreachable sea.

"It's good to talk, isn't it?" she said. "I haven't been able to talk, really talk, in ages."

I didn't disagree.

"You know what they say about rattlesnake, the same as they say about everything, that it tastes no different from chicken. It doesn't. I made it lots of ways, but never got sick of it. Never wanted to eat it again, but never got sick of it."

I nodded and looked at her while she went on in her bikini in the shade with her kids asleep and her husband nowhere nearby.

"You're not like Wolfie," she said, "you're cute."

She reminded me of my ex-stepmother-in-law, Belinda, and not because of her name. Spacey yet earthy, I thought, disregarding the differences between them when I stared at her legs.

No noise came from the bedrooms at night, except for the wheezing of the kids.

"At least they'll get over their colds, but me, I've got no choice but to live with the pain. I shouldn't spend so much time in the hammock, yet it's the only position where my back doesn't hurt. It can't be good for me. Good for me... you'd never believe that a health club wrecked my back. Nothing but good, clean exercise. They sure didn't believe me at the Pain Clinic, I mean — torture victims, amputees, burn survivors — I felt like a phony. Nagging backache: isn't that what you get from watching TV?"

How could she not know who I was? She made me want to confess, but even if I had introduced myself as Ken Honochick instead of as Ken, she probably wouldn't have made the connection. Sports fan or not, she must have seen the commercials, or maybe she joined the club out of boredom. I didn't want to think it was a sincere effort to pull herself out of the stupor, that the goal of air-conditioned self-improvement would have saved her. And I knew better than to hope that the health club in Nadir, Texas, wasn't a branch of Gold Medal Health Spas.

"At the Pain Clinic they said it would never leave, but I could learn to live with it, so Frank took this to mean it was all in my mind. Isn't that just like a man?"

"I can't help feeling responsible."

"Don't be silly," she touched my arm. "Just because I'll always know pain doesn't mean I can't feel pleasure."

I got up to make drinks and she said, "I shouldn't have another," her way of asking for more.

"Where was I - Texas — no, sex. It's not that I can't come — I can and do — it's that there isn't any kind of spasm that doesn't boost the pain. Morality has nothing to do with it. Anyway, Frank would never know unless I told him and then he'd refuse to believe me. Believe me, this isn't the first time I've wanted someone else."

"You're irresistible."

"All dressed up and no place to go," she clinked her glass to mine. "You don't know how wet I am. I could pull down my bottom and you could fuck me through the hammock and in no time I'd come. But the pain — I don't want to think about it."

"Can't I lick you?"

"Makes no difference, it would still end in pain. I could suck you, shit on you, piss on you while you trim my toenails with your teeth, but there's no way."

"Doesn't talking?"

"It's not the same unless you do something, and I know you won't because you're O.K. You don't want to hurt me."

"I can't help thinking how great you'd taste."

"I've had the runs for two days and no bath for a week, but if you promise not to touch, I'll show you my nipples and you can go around the house and jerk off."

This is what the business trip had come to: an offer I couldn't refuse. Although her nipples were no great shakes, I was too worked up not to go through with it.

"Come with me to Seattle and I'll give you more pleasure than you can stand," I couldn't wait to say when I finished.

"Don't be ridiculous."

"I've never known anyone like you. I mean, I've

never had sex like this."

Before she could say no, her kids woke up, so she put the girl in the perpetual motion swing while the boy attacked me.

Wolfie and Frank returned in triumph, having bribed an inspector to update the sticker without looking at the truck. We celebrated with steak and mahi mahi, although cooked together on the grill, neither tasted like itself as much as like the other.

"Can't beat a barbecue," said Frank, recalling the days of snake and Mexico. He didn't quite call it living off the fat of the land.

In the end they couldn't control the rats, yet Frank didn't see how wiping out the rattlesnakes might have turned them loose. He saw nothing beyond how easy it was to sell the ranch. There would always be buyers from some place who wanted to settle down on a snakeless ranch in the middle of nowhere.

"It's a lesson I'll never forget: property sells itself. That's why I got into real estate," he said again, as he had our first night at the airport, with his arm around a beautiful woman and two happy kids draped all over them, not to sell marijuana but to give the secret of his success.

"I should have taken the next plane home," I told Miriam, "but I thought Hawaii couldn't be that bad."

Before we met, I used to see Miriam on the street and nobody could tell me she wasn't special. That was in 1982, and while the agency had given up on me, they couldn't fire me because I was still technically married.

Eventually Miriam and I traded life histories as if we wanted no part of them. Nothing came of it right away, yet we saw enough in each other to want more. I thought her boyfriends were stupid and she didn't argue. Marriage she understood, but to stay with someone as long as I stayed with Jill struck her as unnatural. Miriam thought of time as dog time, where a year shouldn't count for less than seven years, to show how much there was to miss. Although she hadn't yet married Boyd and was more or less unattached, I'm glad we waited.

Those were the glory days of unemployment. With enough severance pay to keep me out of the dumpsters for a few years, I looked forward to life without the agency. They told me not to expect that much as they weaseled out of the contract, which was fine with me. There wouldn't be enough to blow on bad investments, and after the health club scandal my credit rating was a joke. I might have opened a restaurant, but that didn't seem different from working for the agency in Reno. Besides, ex-Sonics from the championship team and ex-Huskies from the Rose Bowl years had first crack at that sort of place, and none of them had made it any bigger than Ernie Steele.

You didn't have to be a football hero to open and operate a decent neighborhood bar, just somebody with sense, gumption, and a tolerance for hard work. Ernie's was the kind of place I loved to visit but could never run.

Other than hang out in bars and cafes, I went to the track and to Tacoma Tigers games, slept late as I pleased and didn't worry about anything. You'd read about the agony some famous ex-jocks in the area went through after there were no more games to play. One lost a job as a TV commentator because he was a stiff, but he didn't enjoy a life of lunch and tennis as much as he did complaining about how he got the shaft. I understood up to a point, but didn't see how a career in broadcasting was going to pull him out of his funk. I thought of calling him and inviting him to a ballgame, but didn't think we'd get along. Besides, he was a lot more famous than I had been and there was a good chance he wouldn't know me.

That was one thing about the promo circuit — even if you didn't recognize another celebrity, you pretended to be pals. A hot shot might dump on a regular person, but he'd treat me like a peer, no matter how small I was compared to him. I didn't keep up with fan magazines. Not knowing who was who, I had to treat people everywhere like they knew me.

This was how I got friendly with Miriam, although in seeing her around town and nodding hello, I couldn't resist putting an extra nudge into my nod. At the Mirror Lounge and the Flame Room, the Dog House and the Five-O we could bump into each other, so it was no surprise to see her outside Longacres.

This was after the feature race and I'd had the kind of day that made me see I would never turn pro. What I lost didn't bother me as much as what I hadn't won. Instead of down fifty, I would have been up three hundred, if only I hadn't frozen on the exacta in the seventh.

I parked on a dead end road across the railroad tracks from the main lot and usually, by the time I returned, the final race hadn't gone off yet. Even if it had, the call wouldn't be clear enough to give away the result, especially when they entered the home stretch to be drowned out by the crowd. The morning paper could print my reprieve, showing how one last fling undid a week's losses. It wasn't strategy — just dumb luck. So far, it hadn't caught up to me.

I never saw why the suckers paid the parking lot a buck to get stuck in traffic, since my free spot was closer to the freeway than any place in the lot was. Others parked on the dead end road and a couple of houses weren't too far away. In other words, you stood a better chance of having your pocket picked under the grandstand than of being mugged out here, but I hadn't counted on what could happen to your car.

Four rickety jacks had the Charger teetering, and even without wheels, the perfectly striped finish and cushy interior told you this was a car that made stripping worth the risk. What were the fifty I'd lost and the three hundred I hadn't won, compared to this?

I didn't want to meet the owner, but there he was... with her. I could have left, if I didn't mind being spotted leaving the scene of the crime the moment he saw his car. Of course, he could have come in one of the old scows and foreign scooters, but this thick-necked brute in a bright knit sports shirt had to be the unlucky one.

He stomped along with the face of a loser, the kind of guy who thought something about her made it impossible for him to concentrate, so that his bad bets were all her fault. She ran so as not to fall behind, then stopped to steady herself on her high heels, and when she saw me and the car she waved before she gasped. He stopped and as the call of the last race echoed through the hills, I couldn't miss my horse's name chasing all the others.

"I didn't see anyone," I said.

He said nothing until I nodded to her: "You know him?"

"No, B.J., I'm only flirting with him so he'll take me home. 'Course I know him, stupe, he's a friend of Wolfie's, only we haven't exactly been introduced."

She wore a lemon tube top and coral tights and even after we said who we were, it didn't feel right to be looking at her as she looked at me. His car wasn't going anywhere, so there was no way out except to offer them a ride.

"Son of a bitch," said B.J., pounding the dash, and although he rattled my speakers, I didn't tell him to stop. "Motherfucking son of a no good bitch."

Miriam sat in back and didn't try to calm him. I knew better than to make conversation, and it was all I could do not to keep checking her in the rearview, to make sure she felt the same as I did. I should have dropped him at a telephone and driven her home, but this wasn't for me to say. After blowing his wad and returning to find his car stripped, no guy wants to have his date go home with another man.

The police station was on the other side of Longacres, which by now was starting to empty, and if we found a cop, he wouldn't be able to do anything for a while. A tow truck wasn't going to help, either. Back at the dead end, it would take no more than a curious push to ruin the exhaust system and inflict a ton of body damage. The nearest gas station was at the freeway, where they'd no doubt sell him ordinary wheels for as much as he'd paid for his mags.

"Don't smoke," he said when I offered him a cigar.

At least you could say he had his health, even if all his beef made him no more than a bulky prop for the paramedics to rehearse *Frankenstein*.

We came to the Aces Wild Card Room, a joint with enough going on so that nobody should have minded waiting here for the cops.

"No, what are you doing," he said when I parked.

"You don't want to call the law?"

"I know where they are — they couldn't be anyplace else."

"Aw, B.J., don't be a palooka," she said. "You gotta report it to collect the insurance, if nothing else."

"Don't go nowhere," he said, getting out and then glancing back the moment we relaxed.

"You're a doll to do this," she said, while he wouldn't quit staring our way.

"I don't suppose you know what he means."

"He doesn't know anything, not even what he doesn't know."

"Empire," he said, like I was no more than a hack. Still, it made sense to cruise the junkyards, since he could pick up another set of wheels or even recover his own if the thieves had unloaded them in one of the scrap shops on Empire Way.

"If it's not one, it'll be the other," he said.

The first one wasn't open. That didn't keep him from pounding the door until the dogs came.

"6:30 on a Sunday — he doesn't expect much, does he?"

"Mr. Easy Does It, or hadn't you noticed?"

A gate kept him from the dogs, but one got in a harmless nip.

"You want a piece of me, you motherfucking son of a no good bitch?"

He led with his left, then came around with the right when the dog took the bait, smashing the fence loud enough to ring over the barking, but no: that was the alarm.

"Poor B.J.," she gave him a lipstick-smudged hankie for his hand, which bled like it wouldn't clot.

Nobody driving by seemed to notice as we left the noise behind. Between a tetanus shot and death by lockjaw stood no more than one more yard.

Miriam whispered quickly as he stomped to the gate, "Listen, you're going to think I'm rotten for this, but there's no way I'm going home with him."

"Not really, I'd think you were rotten if you did go home with him."

"What I mean is, I'm bailing, but not without your help."

The dogs, the smashing, and the alarm didn't take as long this time.

Without any more junkyards to look forward to, there was hope he'd get out at the next emergency room.

"Where the fuck do you think you're going?" he said as I headed for the hospitals and then told me not to bother.

"Just take me back to the car," he said, although we were no closer to where we had been than to where we were going.

"I'm going to Capitol Hill; if that's not good enough, I'll drop you along the way," I said, as the way turned into a part of town a chunky white guy with a diplomacy problem shouldn't visit when he was on his best behavior.

He stared, he blinked, he did not begin to comprehend, let alone decide. Maybe he had no friends to drive him around and I was the best he could come up with.

Miriam said we should just go home, kissing him on the neck like she wasn't going to ditch him, but at the next light she bolted. By the time I drove across the intersection, she had disappeared into one of a row of stores.

He went after her, holding her hankie like a gentleman on an errand to return it as he lunged after her, into a place she wouldn't have been by the time he got through the crowd, and I slipped back into the traffic.

My way of doing things was not his way, and what had my way done for me? By tomorrow his car would be off and rolling, but what of my failed marriage, my lost job, the pitiless flop of my so-called career? I was nobody to deny him the chance to do things for himself. Taking action might even work for him — much better than not getting involved had worked for me.

He was no genius, but he was bright enough to hold a job that bought a nice car. As for him and Miriam, maybe it was no more than a case of opposites attract.

"You're welcome," I had said, not feeling entirely unsympathetic as he slammed the door and shouted.

"Thanks for nothing!"

In the spring of 1982 the agency finally came up with a gig that was supposed to be not my downfall but the beginning of my comeback. If I could sing, it might have worked, but I couldn't sing, dance, or tell jokes. Not that talent mattered as much as looks in any of their schemes.

They wanted me to look the way I did when I was famous and they wanted Jill to lose ten pounds, even though she wasn't overweight. Before she could say no, the agency changed its plans. To begin with, they wanted us to look not younger but older, to gain weight and dress like middle Americans, to be extremely average.

Although it wasn't mentioned, we were being groomed for an ad blitz that ployed the oldest scam in the New World: the Fountain of Youth. Jill and I were chosen because we weren't so old that we couldn't be made to look young. They wouldn't say how we'd go backward through the stages, only that surgery had nothing to do with it. We should have known that it amounted to no more than a cure for baldness.

It ended before it began — not because the product wouldn't work. And we couldn't have hoped for a more spectacular return to the limelight. Jill, though, couldn't see how she fit in. She walked out, so the agency no longer had to bother with me. I was too negative. As the saying goes, if I was accused of being a salesman, there'd be no evidence to convict me.

I didn't blame Jill for leaving and, in a way, she did us both a favor. Those who wondered why it took us so long to split had never made a six-figure salary for appearing to be happily married. Why we split was no mystery, either. Jill saved while I spent, so she had taken all she could from our marriage, making it crazy for her not to leave.

While neither of us had much use for nostalgia, I needed the Nostalgia Show more than she did. Jill said she'd do it for old times, not for me but for her father.

You couldn't call the Nostalgia Show a failure. Many didn't like life as they found it and wanted to go back to the way it had been. I had been — no, was — stationed between the Woodstock Diorama and the Moon Booth. I didn't mind that they hadn't put me in the sports section. After all, I wasn't Mark Spitz. My medals didn't match his, neither did my hair. I wasn't as handsome and my wife wasn't as beautiful, but I was here and he wasn't, even if he was their first choice.

Instead of sticking me with the ballplayers signing autographs for unbelievable sums, they put me over a tank of water on a platform spring-loaded to a target. They had glued on a flesh-colored bathing cap to make me look hopelessly bald. The people got two balls for a dollar, which they paid without complaints because the money went to charity.

The trouble with nostalgia at an early age is that people aren't so feeble that they can't throw. It was softball season and nobody missed.

By noon I was undone, dazed and confused, my medals tangled around my neck. They weren't the actual medals. Those were on display at agency headquarters, but these were no less heavy, lead for gold.

The water smelled no better than if would have if the installers had used it for a toilet. Aside from the medals and cap, I wore the stars and stripes, although you couldn't tell since my belly folded over the tank suit.

They hadn't told Jill how to dress, but they should have told her what not to wear. She wore the most offensive outfit she could, which made no sense except as a protest against all the show was about and all her father had ever made her do as my partner in promotions. Nobody knew how to take it when Jill came up grinning in a pink suit and pillbox hat that was a dead ringer for what Jackie Kennedy wore at the event which, more than anything here, defined our collective past.

"Don't be shy, step right up folks and bang the Olympian," a man from the agency barked to distract the crowd from being menaced by my wife.

While the Woodstock Diorama played a tape of Ten Years After and the Moon Booth put on the soundtrack from *2001*, a live band started nowhere we could see, so to us everything was out of time. It was supposed to be rhythm and blues, songs nobody could mistake. There was a jumbled clapping and stomping for dancing and the singer sounded like a black man, but this was black music for white people, featuring tune, not beat. In a place built for basketball, it was no more than noise.

The Woodstock hippies chanted NO MORE RAIN and the salesmen sons of astronauts told how their fathers had found space travel to be "not unlike experiencing an hallucinogenic drug."

To reach the men's room I went through rows of tie-dye and patchouli, old comic books and baseball cards, record albums, black light posters, and hash pipes, yet in my tank suit, flip flops, and fake medals I went unnoticed. They'd come for fun, for a soft look back at what might have been: nobody wanted to remember the Munich Olympics.

I couldn't avoid the sports section any longer. Then I saw that the organizers of the show did me a favor in not putting me among the former ballplayers, bowlers, and hydroplane drivers, since all of them looked in better shape than I was. Those whose sport is a game don't think of play as work, but swimmers think of swimming pools another way.

None seemed to see me until I left, when one did a double-take and gave me the once-over. He wore the hat of the Seattle Pilots and the shirt of the Seattle Mariners, so even though I didn't recognize him, I knew who he was.

"You'll never guess who's headed this way," the barker crowed when he saw who followed me.

"No," I did my bit as I climbed to the platform, "not Diego Segui!"

We met on the coliseum floor, only I wasn't on the floor but over a tank of dirty water. Some might say the career of a journeyman pitcher didn't compare to a gold medal in the Olympics, that to be the best in the world at anything, if only for a moment, was the supreme athletic accomplishment. Everyone watched him, not me. Those who didn't know him were told by those who did, as in the game show Jeopardy, where the answer is the question. Diego Segui: who was the only guy to play not only for the Pilots but also for the Mariners?

He couldn't ignore me any longer. He seemed to recognize what I had done with a wave of his pitching arm, but his backstroke formed a wind-up and to look at his face was to think he had never retired. He wasn't as large as some of the throwers, but he threw with his legs. He put his weight behind the arm and when he let fly I didn't see him land as much as imagine the glove up, in position for a line drive up the middle.

The crack of the wood, the muffled roar of the crowd, and the sight of Jill feeling Diego's muscle kept me under as long as I could stand not to breathe. My view was from the movie where we identified with the graduate at the bottom of a pool in scuba gear, who didn't know what to do with his life.

In the rush for air, I bumped the splintered target,

triggering an ungodly nosebleed. Was I the only one
here who hadn't been drinking beer for hours?
Although the target was gone and the game was over,
they had no fear of escalation.

After Diego Segui came a man who could have been
a general with all his decorations, except his uniform
was a bowling shirt and his ball wasn't a baseball. The
footwork began and the people not only watched, but
made way. I could have been an electronic blip on a
video screen, doomed to intersect with nothing worse
than another blip. Spun marble mesmerized me, stretching the instant as I pulled myself to the platform
through the shattering of an explosion no softer than the
rush of water. The target zone became the only safe
place in a room flowing with glass on a film that didn't
keep from running into moon shots and rock festivals.

Fist fights broke out like there was no tomorrow.
Hippies tore through the paper flower walls of their
diorama to invade the sons of astronauts, who couldn't
hit back from inside their space suits, but couldn't be
hurt much, either. Dispirited, inspired, or desperate,
the organizers played a tape of John Lennon and Yoko
Ono singing "Give Peace a Chance." Murder had transformed Lennon from buffoon to sage since the days
when he was a great rock star, and those who resented
Ono for whatever reason now felt for her, yet the fighting wouldn't stop.

So this was Seattle, mellow Seattle, where a month
earlier Jill and I were to resume our career as though
Reno or even Denver hadn't made our marriage irrelevant. Facing a future of divorce and unemployment in a
violent city, I should have been miserable. I wasn't: I
was relieved.

-5

"We're friends, aren't we Chick? That won't be a problem?"

"What won't?"

She wouldn't say. It was November, 1987, the end of free rent and the beginning of a trip Miriam planned to the Big Island via the Biggest Little City in the World, even if I wasn't thrilled about returning to Reno.

"We'll win so much that we'll never look back," she said among the sidewalk piles set out for sale or garbage day.

German cars circled the block because there was no place to park. We smiled at their owners, and when they walked their dogs they never failed to wrap the turds in plastic.

After weeks of burst pipes and clogged toilets, nobody wanted to stay in that building. We looked forward to moving, even though the air had that sunless dank chill that made you not want to go outside. To see our rucksacks and sleeping bags, you would have thought we were going to some rugged destination like Mt. Rainier or Glacier instead of a city that never slept.

The ex-tenants couldn't help liking Miriam. That didn't stop envy or resentment. She could have kicked them out long ago for not paying rent instead of telling them to fix their own plumbing. She hadn't made all the money she could have and yet she was the only one of us hitting the road with a wad of travelers' checks. She still had her looks, and if that wasn't enough, she had me. Why is it that people with nothing covet what those with next to nothing have, ignoring those who have it all?

We should have left, but stayed, as if we were trying to sell the toaster to a man whose car we couldn't have had for all the value of a condemned building. It made no sense to say good-bye.

"Who cares if we don't make Hawaii," she said. "We could buy that farm in Texas, play the ponies in Hialeah...there's nothing we can't do."

Miriam couldn't drive. I thought that wouldn't matter — get on the interstate and a chimp could drive — but it did. That wasn't all she held back. She refused to say how much she had or how much I could pretend was mine, only that it wasn't enough.

What we expected from each other wasn't easy to explain. It would have been wrong to say "I love you" but to say "I don't love you" would have been worse than wrong. Opening doors for her, driving, carrying her bags, lighting her smokes was a good start, but we wouldn't say what we wanted from each other or from the trip. Most of all, we didn't talk about recovering what we had lost; we talked about winning.

Sweating against my skin were what the agency returned to me unasked the moment the contract died. The ribbons pinched, but I kept them on, and not because Miriam had put them there. It had been a while since I'd worn them and I didn't want to lose them. Not a good attitude for Reno.

"You aren't going to welsh, are you Chick?"

"Don't tell me you want a contract."

"No babe, you know."

"Isn't a promise enough?"

She shook her head and I couldn't deny her, even if I hadn't taken her seriously when she found them dangling from a door knob. She couldn't have thought I'd have left them behind any more than I should have thought she was only teasing when she said I owed her one.

Slipping a hand into my shirt, I pulled a ribbon overhead and, without taking my foot off the brake or the car out of Drive, I draped the gold around her neck and kissed her.

"No, Chick, it's, it's..."

"It's not a gift."

Jill didn't want to leave Reno, even if she could see why I had to do what the International Olympic Committee said. In the months it took Roger Patterson to regain control of the agency, there was no way the I.O.C. wouldn't find us. We weren't so much criminals on the lam as unruly kids who knew they had it coming.

The letter threatening to strip me of my medals wasn't a running joke, regardless of how many times it came or which new signature was at the bottom. There was the usual whine about the Olympic ideal, but they never failed to presume my innocence and integrity. They didn't doubt I'd fix everything.

I couldn't have been the only one who got these letters. Maybe in some unofficial standings I led the pack. I never really got used to them. After all, I had done worse than play pro football, and if a hero like Jim Thorpe could be stripped, why not me? I didn't keep in touch with my old teammates and never ran into ex-Olympians on the promo circuit. Did other medallists make more for doing even less, or should I have been ashamed because many who worked harder to achieve more had ended up in no better than regular jobs where they worked harder to make less?

Jill and I couldn't have asked for a sweeter deal than what we got in Reno, even if neither of us gambled. What could gambling mean to people on unlimited expense accounts? We had to play the tables on the job, but the money wasn't for keeping.

It was after the '80 Olympics, when the president didn't let Americans win medals in Moscow that they could parlay into gold at home. I should have felt sorry for those who had traded their teenage years for a shot at being best in the world, but I knew nothing in Munich could stack up to anything won by an American in Moscow: their loss was my gain.

People at the Abracadabra didn't care about sports they couldn't bet on, which suited the agency. It was to be no more than a runway for us, to take off for something better.

The Abracadabra wasn't downtown, and had no other casinos nearby. It had been built in no time out of nothing in the middle of nowhere, as if by magic. It milked the theme of mirage, right down to having the cocktail waitresses wear no clothes.

I didn't know who ran the place and assumed it was the mob. The agency told me not to worry about any of that, but it was hard not to complain when they took me off V.I.P. duty in order to make me a lifeguard.

You couldn't blame them: an Olympic lifeguard for an Olympic-sized pool. And wasn't the basic stroke of the rescuer the backstroke? They didn't care that I didn't know CPR, but they did expect me to show off a few times each day. A flutter kick here, a flip turn there: nothing your basic Marineland seal couldn't handle. They thought I'd be flattered, but they were wrong, and I thought I'd hate it, but I was mistaken. It wouldn't have been bad, except for the lessons.

Rich men paid me to teach their kids how to swim, and while I didn't need the money, the agency said this was part of the job. The kids acted wise, said the backstroke wasn't really swimming, that real swimming was the Australian crawl. I didn't tell them to crawl back to Australia; I told them that backward was the way of giant squids. As an underhand softball pitch was less unnatural (and faster) than an overhand hardball throw, the backstroke let the arms do what they were made to do. Plus, you didn't have to think about breathing. If they complained about smacking into the end of the pool, though, I had no answer. After thousands of laps, with or without the overhead signal flags, you might think a guy would have a sense for the end. If I wasn't thinking, I'd forget.

Sooner or later, the father would take me aside and ask how the kid was, meaning not how he was doing but whether he had any talent. With a little work, couldn't the kid turn into a champion? The little work was shrugged off like nothing and the championships didn't stop in the pools of the NCAA.

What surprised me was that it wasn't hard to spare them grief by telling them the truth. First, though, I gave the line that work could overcome anything (you couldn't deny it any more than believe it). Just as unbelievable would have been the line that the kid had no chance, no matter how much closer this was to the truth. Almost nobody can hit water and flat out move. Fewer still can do it like they never want to stop. Out of three dozen kids, one might have had a shot, but for him

I put it no differently than for the others, except to adjust the odds.

"Not bad," I told the old man, "maybe as good as 40-1."

"40-1 not bad!"

"Even Spitz wasn't a lock at the very beginning. It's no different from the future book of the Derby: a lot can go wrong."

"What do you really think, though?" he said, unlike the others, who'd heard worse than 100-1.

Obviously, he didn't back longshots. For some, who had inherited money or had it come easy, a longshot wouldn't have been a bad sort of quest. Anyone could pump up the value of amateur athletics by telling himself that, if nothing else, the kid would learn self-discipline. For others, who had made fortunes by taking risks, 40-1 might have seemed no worse than the going rate of success. Not this guy.

"What I want to know is," he gripped my arm, "wasn't it worth it?"

At the edge of the pool in the middle of a desert in a late afternoon of August, it felt like everyone was listening, even though not even his son was around. We both wore sunglasses, yet I could see his eyes: I couldn't look away and he wouldn't let go. Anyone watching from a balcony might have thought he wanted to hit me, but I hadn't cheated him and there was no way to get out of this by lying. He wasn't going to take a wisecrack for an answer.

To look at us, you would pick not me but him for the ex-jock. Did he once have a 40-1 shot at going all the way in some sport, but for some reason didn't take it? I couldn't tell him what his son should do with the next eight years. If we boycotted the Russians' Olympics, why shouldn't they boycott ours? Unless you beat them, you couldn't call yourself the best of anything, and it could go on like that forever, making gold cheaper than roulette chips. You could waste your life chasing medals you couldn't pawn for wine.

"I can't say yes," I said.

He nodded, but when he turned away, I saw he took this to mean "no."

I wasn't the only ex-jock on the payroll, but I was the only one that didn't play golf. Even the ex-boxer, with his blurred vision and brain damage, couldn't fail to hit the ball, although his stumbling was an act to make others think he was easy meat.

The ex-boxer had no agency. Not that he needed one: someone had set him up in the casino as a kind of pension. We didn't call him Champ because he'd never been one. Instead of Number Three, his highest ranking, he called himself Basie because he couldn't count how many times he'd been down. And yet he boasted of never having gone into the ring when he didn't know who would win. He said it so naturally, you thought he couldn't have been bragging about taking dives.

We waited in the bar while the boss arranged matches, and you could tell the boss wished he had nothing but boxers and ballplayers to match with the V.I.P.s. If the V.I.P.s took them for long lost fathers, I was the cousin they never knew they had.

Life for the ballplayers wasn't exactly carefree. Unlike the I.O.C., the baseball commissioner wasted no time banning them from the game for getting paid by a casino to play golf. It happened to Mantle and Mays, so there was no way it wouldn't happen to Nipsy and Spike.

Getting banned from baseball wasn't the same as

having your medals stripped. They still had their
records and they weren't about to mail in their trophies.
All it meant was, while they worked here they couldn't
"associate" with any team. No team could put them on
the payroll. Not that any team would pay them as much
as the casino did to play golf.

Nipsy, the ex-shortstop from Mexico, didn't care,
but Spike, the ex-slugger from Arkansas, made a stink
about his inalienable rights. In other words, he had bud-
dies in positions to give him jobs in the game while
Nipsy didn't.

They weren't hard to get along with, even if they
asked what I was doing here. Nobody said anything that
wasn't meant to tease. Deep down, though, we knew we
weren't on anyone's first string of ex-jocks. Even when
strangers came up to Spike and mentioned some ball
he'd hit that "hadn't come down yet," he pretended it
was nothing. This wasn't false modesty because he
knew what they really remembered. Years ago he'd cost
his team a title by making an incredibly stupid play.
People called him Spike to his face, but behind his back
he would always be known as Skull, short for
Numbskull, and although it was one thing about his
career that nobody could forget, Spike didn't have to tell
us not to tease him about it.

The bar was the only part of the Abracadabra
where the drinks weren't free. We didn't pay, but in
order to spend time away from the tables, the customers paid plenty. Basie got more than his share of
glances, since he wore enough jewelry to blow out an
airport full of gun detectors, yet he couldn't say he'd
won the jewels prize fighting. He'd won them playing
golf, only to him, it wasn't play.

We kidded Basie by saying how the V.I.P.s would get
even: two fat executives would sit on him so he could-

n't get up while the Chairman of the Board mashied his ribs with a niblick.

The cocktail waitresses scolded us for being rowdy, but the boss coached us not to be restrained. There was a rule about the waitresses though, no matter what these women said. "Easy, Count, save some for the late rounds," and "Nipsy can pick it, but Spike can really drive you home," and "You stroke my back, I'll stroke yours," were their ways of telling us not to fuck up.

They didn't tell us not to get drunk. Maybe they figured we wouldn't work and good help was hard to find. We didn't drink as much as we might have; it would have kept us from rehearsing.

From the way we rehearsed, you would have thought nothing mattered as much as getting into one of those ex-jock beer commercials. We loved the ads and knew all the lines by heart, and if the rehearsals were a little pathetic, we couldn't quit, because of Spike.

Like Nipsy and Basie, Spike had no agent. Unlike them, he begged me to get the agency to give us a try-out. We tried to tell him it wouldn't work. He couldn't use the ads as a forum to get back into baseball. He pretended to agree, but there was no stopping him. The agency had its own ideas and the brewery had its own agency and nobody got paid as much as they did to write what would be said.

In front of a camera I was still a stiff, so I had no worry about getting picked. Nipsy could field lines like he could field line drives, but he wasn't infamous enough to sell America beer. Basie was hopeless: if you weren't used to his mumble, you couldn't understand him. But the agency knew what they wanted, and it wasn't a mishmash of unknown has-beens. They didn't even need an audition. They came with a truckload of lights and cameras for no other purpose than to make a commercial.

They paid actors to be extras because, unknown as we were, we were known enough to distract viewers with an inkling that they knew us from somewhere, which would distort the focus. The focus was on Spike, so he should have been satisfied, but there couldn't be "tastes great" without "less filling." To millions, he was none other than Skull. That he hit .290 and drove in 100 runs for a team that finished a game behind the best team in the league didn't matter. All that mattered was that once in his life he didn't look where he was going. He hadn't killed anyone. He'd even hit a ball that should have won the game and the pennant, but it didn't. The announcer said any numbskull should have known the runner had to wait until it was clear that the ball would-n't be caught. And Spike should have known why a big time beer wanted to put him on national TV, yet not until he signed the contract did he see what was up.

"Hiya, Skull, long time no see."

Nobody but an ex-teammate could have called him that; the only one who would was Ewell Hoskin, the man he'd run into on the last play of a season he'd sent to hell.

Spike wouldn't smile. In those days of uninflated salaries, the World Series share he'd denied his team-mates wasn't just a pat on the back.

"Mule, I...I can't say how sorry — "

"Forget it, Skull, no sweat."

There was nothing we could do. Spike had so little to recite, he couldn't pretend to forget his lines. When my agency thanked me for finding him, I didn't say "you're welcome." The brewery agency promised to use me sometime, while I tried not to tell them what I thought about their cheap shot.

You couldn't say they didn't know their stuff, though. The extras didn't miss a beat and Ewell the Mule

went down the bar looking up just as everyone remembered, not ordering a beer but waiting for a ball to drop.

When Spike didn't move, the director told him to
think of it as a chance to make up for the past by pok-
ing fun at it, while the boss tried to persuade Ewell to
join the casino staff.

"No way — think I want to be banned from the
game?"

Only Spike didn't laugh.

"Great line," said the director, "not today, but for the
next one."

"Next one?" said Spike, as if it hadn't occurred to
him.

"This has series potential," said the director, "can't
miss."

"Yeah, Skull, this is one shot at a series we won't
blow."

Spike couldn't wait for his cue. When he crashed
into Hoskin it was no less than another awful memory,
right down to the crack of bone.

"Cut" wasn't necessary. There wasn't going to be a
series or even another take.

Reno gives no first impression. By the time you visit a
gambling city, so many movies and stories have covered
the territory, what you see comes off as no closer than
secondhand. Not that this cheapens the thrill.

I wanted to concentrate on what we were good at
and not leave ourselves open to the diversions of lights,
bells, rattles, and screams, so we went to a room where
they took bets on horse races at tracks around the country. Miriam couldn't stay put.

"Can't you feel the energy?" she said.

I said we needed a set of rules so we wouldn't go

crazy. We would go where she wanted to go and do nothing she didn't want to do, after we spent an hour here. Even then, we wouldn't rush off to the Abracadabra.

My old cohorts wouldn't be there, anyway. Spike had left before I did and I heard Nipsy went back to Mexico, but it was hard not to picture Basie in Reno, Tahoe, or Vegas.

"She liked it here, didn't she?"

I had told Miriam a little about Jill, but she never really asked about her.

"Won't you tell me what she was like?"

"She wasn't like Barbie."

"And you weren't like Ken."

I couldn't believe she wanted to talk about my ex-wife here and now. We sat in the Cal-Neva race book room, juggling editions of the *Daily Racing Form* from New York, Chicago, and California, and trying to unravel Nevada's four-digit listing system of entries with everything going off at once. The fifth at Hawthorne jumped the gate while we tried not to miss the doubles in the West and the house trifecta based on the nightcap at Aqueduct.

"She wasn't like you, either."

"That's not the question."

It was below zero in Chicago and, like iron horses, the animals on satellite TV puffed white clouds into the clear blue distance while results from Philly and Hialeah came over the ticker and the intercom gave a late scratch in Shreveport, but Jill deserved more than a glib put-down in the middle of a casino, no matter when the cut-off was for Hollywood.

"Didn't we have that one?" I said as the Chicago horse we forgot to bet on won easily.

Miriam wasn't paying attention. We were no more used to the scene than we had been when we walked in.

Maybe the trick in dealing with too much at once was to screen it all out by talking about something off the subject, but what was there to say about my ex that wouldn't sell her short?

"I guess she wasn't much different from any pretty girl with a media power broker for a father, but as she grew up he pushed her into gigs she didn't want to do. It was payback time for all those Easter egg hunts on the estates of movie stars, those insider tours of Disneyland, the birthday parties of endless presents. She didn't start out shy and she even adjusted to the pressure, but after a while she couldn't face the face time."

"Wasn't she some kind of queen?"

"She never should have done it, even if she was kind of flattered. I mean, who wouldn't want to be Queen of the Roses?"

We blew the double at Bay Meadows by confusing it with the one at Hollywood, which didn't go off until a half hour later. The wins you thought you should have won didn't count except for aggravation. There were too many races and not enough moments between them. It wasn't like going to the track. It was too fast and not fast enough, like a strobe light slicing what you thought you saw quickly into slow motion.

After we left the race book room we said no more about Jill. The air had a dry, icy sting we hadn't known in Seattle. The street seemed crisp and clean in the sun, until we saw how a dome of smog enclosed us among the casinos, souvenir shops, churches, and schools, so it was just as well our nostrils pinched involuntarily to keep us from breathing.

I hadn't lived here long enough to get to know the outside. The agency wanted us to settle in a neighborhood apart from the action, but neither Jill nor I saw the point, after that cleancut ghetto in Colorado. Now

Miriam couldn't get over how I had to ask directions to the post office.

The mountain view was a nice change from the gambling halls the way taking a leak was a nice change from not taking a leak. We weren't ready yet for the tables. We didn't know craps, and Keno was glorified Bingo. As horseplayers, we wanted no part of roulette, and that went double for the machines.

As for poker, these grim sessions weren't the game I knew. Either the players were very good, in which case you didn't belong there, or they were ordinary, which meant they didn't go in for razzle dazzle. It seemed to be a point of etiquette not to smile when you won. Just rake it in and show how you didn't care. The house dealt and got a piece of the pot and the games were set in advance, so you couldn't play anything wild, like Night Baseball in the Rain.

By default or disqualification, we fell into blackjack. Although we weren't card counters, we knew the percentages: when to split, when to double down, whether to hit or stand and never to take insurance. Above all, we knew the bottom line: this was a negative expectation proposition. The house advantage was slim yet undeniable. You couldn't win in the long run, but you could get lucky. The trick was not to push it.

Blackjack never stopped. As we went from casino to casino, we noticed how the roulette wheels and crap shooters took a break now and then and the poker pits seemed to be empty more often than not. With blackjack, there were always dealers ready and not once did we enter a gambling hall where someone wasn't waiting for the next card.

House rules varied, but you could sit almost anywhere and not face a shoe containing a bunch of shuffled decks. Bottom limits went down to a dollar and the unstated top limit made it seem that you could push out a few thousand at the end of a single deck game at a bottom limit table. This, of course, would mark you as a card counter, and you'd be lucky not to get bounced. Betting as if you kept track mentally of the discards was even illegal. It was impossible to prove and some had challenged the law, but it had been upheld that a casino could throw you out for winning.

Never mind that books on how to count cards were great for business, that for every savant who could keep his mind on the system there had to be hundreds of scatterbrains. As far as we were concerned, their rules didn't apply. We joined games in progress and left before they saw we had no pattern.

No session ended with us losing more than a hundred. We had no base bet. We didn't play progressions as much as whims. Nobody says you have to face a fresh deck, but shuffling didn't stop us. We didn't hope for tens and aces for ourselves as much as for the dealer to get stuck with dregs, and often we won by standing below seventeen while the dealer busted himself.

We took turns holding hands: Miriam didn't play against men and I didn't play against women. We wouldn't explain this any more than we needed to. Nothing mattered but success, even if success was just a few days off from a career of failure.

We didn't buy chips. Walk up to a game/ plop down cash/ win or lose/ leave without trying to get even kept us away from the free drinks. We didn't spend a lot of time watching a game before we jumped in; when we did, we noticed how people mostly beat themselves. By moving around, we didn't cut into the house advantage the way a card counter might, but we didn't split it wide open the way these pattern freaks did when they tried to do everything right.

We didn't celebrate. We had the $2.99 all-you-can-eat buffet and grabbed a cheap room when rooms went on sale at whatever hotel we might be passing through, so our daily expenses never amounted to what we might lose on a single hand.

It didn't take long to see there was no use. We couldn't make more than we'd ever need. We were too young to retire and too old to work for nothing but a chance to play. We had made more than enough to get to Hawaii and Hawaii didn't matter any more. Neither did Reno. The food was bland, the rooms were no different from hotel to hotel, the beauty of the casinos blended and lulled. It almost got so we looked for disorder — outbursts of losers, fights between drunks, women trying to claw their men away from the pits — anything for a laugh.

"Weren't we going to use the money for a trip to the Big Island?" I said.

I didn't want to go to any island, so this was a jinx to make sure we wouldn't. In a way, Hawaii was no different from Nevada. Whether you're flopping on a beach or kicking ass at the tables, the fun itself never lives up to the prospect of having fun. Not that we were about to deposit our roll in the nearest bank and set out to build a place for ourselves in a community of steady jobs. Closer to forty than thirty, we didn't need to read the latest life expectancy charts to know we were far from done, and we'd come too far to waste any more time trying to beat the house in order to make it to paradise.

"I thought you said we wouldn't," she said.

"It won't hurt to look."

We had made our last bet and decided not to push

it. While this stop was an exception, there was no guarantee we wouldn't get sucked back in.

Maybe it wouldn't be there. Hadn't fires destroyed other casino hotels? Like World's Fair pavilions, these plaster castles didn't have to scream come-and-get-it to the bulldozers. Built for the moment instead of eternity, a casino could be flattened, renovated, bought and sold without anyone noticing.

The odds were, no matter what we found, we would think it was ridiculous. After upsetting the tables and rejecting the lure, we were disenchanted, but there it was: the Abracadabra.

I didn't know if we had broken through the dome of smog, but the light was more golden, the sky bluer, the mountains immaculately whiter. Even if you didn't pull over to behold the sight of this casino so removed from the others that the whole desert was its property, the long drive on an uncluttered highway made the Abracadabra a goal.

Jill and I hadn't paid much attention to anything but what the agency flack told us when the limo first brought us here. Besides, the view through smoked glass wasn't the same.

To impress gamblers who were used to the standard casino flash, the management spared nothing to display the extraordinary. In 1980 as now, the Abracadabra made a statement that no other place would do. That wasn't easy. In the casino racket, a hyped-gimmick motif was the rule, not the exception.

In a way, it didn't work. Like a brand of beer or cigarettes that tries to pass itself off as a cut above the ordinary while delivering no better than the usual taste, the Abracadabra was all image. Your chance of winning was no greater here than anywhere else; neither was the food. The usual perks and courtesies might have seemed special here, but if cash didn't crash into chips fast enough, a gambling hall went out of business. The positive attraction of a grand entrance also posed a negative. Nobody wanted to drive all the way out here. The free shuttle service helped, but the other casinos didn't stop the rumor that it was only free one way.

But no outsider could tell how a casino did, particularly a casino whose shtick was illusion. Did they hire ex-jocks because they were desperate for drawing cards or wasn't this another sign of swank?

This time in the afternoon at the end of the year the sun couldn't wait to set. Although it wasn't yet dark, the moment we turned into the surprisingly full parking lot, search lights shot upward.

"Some things don't change," I said.

"Suppose there isn't a prize fight, that this is business as usual?"

"There might be, but it is," I said, and if I sounded disappointed, it was because we stood a better chance at beating the slots than at running into Basie. The search lights were no indication that anything unusual was happening.

Until we stepped outside.

Attendants on camelback directed us through sphinxes along the path from the car to the lobby. Suddenly air around us warmed and even though I had lived here, the giant glass pyramid ceiling gave me the sense of walking into a wonderful new space. A maze of hallways became game rooms brighter than daylight and louder than wind. Towering minarets and glowing domes drew off the smokes of roast garlic lamb. Long pools led through courtyards of gardens, each more beautiful than the other, and we moved through the arcades with a purpose, pausing to admire. All was ours to inspect and enjoy.

With everywhere open to us, we followed a red carpet that seemed to be there because we were there. Could they have remembered me? The cocktail waitresses were sleek and tender. The dealers and pit bosses were friendly and kind. Even the crapshooters smiled. Everyone was happy, charming, debonair, handsome, and well dressed. The laughter was music. There was music! People welcomed us. We belonged. We were as exciting and attractive as they were.

"No, no, no, cut, CUT for chrissakes. They're not Tom and Melanie!"

Everyone groaned and looked at us like we'd done the unforgivable.

"Behind the rope, with the crowd," said a guy so big, he didn't have to be polite.

Then we saw the cameras, the rope holding back those who didn't wear suits and gowns. We crossed the line where the smiles of the chic met the stares of the desperate as they tried to look like they weren't ugly.

"Wouldn't you know," I said, "another commercial."

"Not a commercial," whispered one of the crowd, "a movie."

-4

"Don't you just hate the movies?" she said.

"I never go any more."

"I used to think the old ones weren't so bad. Then a magazine had reviewers give their top tens, and you'll never guess which movie topped every all-time list."

"Not *Citizen Kane*."

"Not even close: *It's a Wonderful Life*."

We were almost out of Utah, where we hadn't stopped except for gas.

"*Casablanca, Gone with the Wind, Lawrence of Arabia* — nothing but clichés," she said.

"*Lawrence of Arabia* wasn't so bad."

"Oh no? Tell me it wasn't dick worship."

It was freezing and dry, without snow. We couldn't put off the question of what was next because it was too late for baseball and the wrong time of year to be driving across the Rockies. We should have gone south, but Miriam wanted no part of Mexico.

"I wouldn't make a movie top ten any more than I'd make a list of my favorite dogs," she said.

Size and looks didn't matter as much as disposition,

but when you had time to kill, everything mattered a little. It became an in/out list rather than a top-to-bottom order, with neither of us picking a number one and both down-grading non-Boston terriers. Getting out of Utah wasn't a snap, after all.

If Mexico was out, nobody but a lunatic would have gone north. Miriam had lived in Oakland, which disqualified California. She didn't want to go where she used to live, and she had lived so many places that I knew more about her taste in dogs than I did about what she had been through. I didn't think much about going back to where I used to live, but she came to think of nothing else.

We had different reasons for not wanting to relive the past and similar ones for not wanting to avoid it. My reasons weren't as good as hers because my past was better. Her past was so bad, she never mentioned it; mine was so good, I was ashamed. Not of what I had done; of what I had become. I didn't mention this, in case I had become no better than all she had ever been. What a pair: no wonder we rated *The Maltese Falcon* lower than the Norwegian elk hound.

Anything beat talking about what happened in Denver, but Interstate 70 made no detour.

Ready or not, here we were.

Compared to Denver, the casino gig and the Nostalgia Show were hopeless tries to salvage something from disaster. As with the other agency "can't miss" projects, I did what they wanted, even if they had doubts about their use for me after the spa fiasco. Whether in the spirit of never-say-die or in the rut of a bad habit, they made Jill's father our direct account executive. Officially, he had resigned; unofficially, he accepted the demotion. After all, the promo had almost nothing to do with me and almost everything to do with my wife.

Over the years, Jill had learned that she didn't like being a star, yet she perversely suffered spasms of attraction for the stage. Maybe she had to draw attention to herself in some embarrassing public act just to punish her father, who, worse than denying his mistakes, kept trying to correct them.

We lived in an apartment that could have been anywhere, so as not to appear out of the ordinary. We had to follow a story that said an injury wouldn't let me train for triathlons. It was absurd, but I was glad not to take part in celebrity tennis tournaments with Broncos and Nuggets.

The agency was ambivalent about the lawsuits, as if there really was no such thing as bad publicity, while the lawyers told us not to talk about the health club. We were to act sorry and not carry on like we expected to beat the rap. Not only that, we had to court sympathy. Shortly after arriving in Denver, Jill and I found that sympathy couldn't be bought merely with the pain of faked injury. The typical vengeful consumers were right to want more after what we, however indirectly, had done to them.

"Don't say anything until I finish," said Roger Patterson, who'd taken us not to the fanciest restaurant but to a steakhouse where clatter and sizzle made everyone loud. It was the perfect place not to be overheard. "Even then, think about it and don't answer until tomorrow.

"Think of me not as Dad but as Boss; or not as Boss but as one of the team. We're all in this together, aren't we? Or, Ken — Jill, darling, you haven't finished your T-bone — Ken, my man, Jill, sweetheart, what would you say is the biggest trend going down today, numero uno, bar none?"

"Not triathlons," I groaned.

"You don't say! No no no, BIG. We're at the gateway to the eighties here — not disco, not revolution, none of your flings with Eastern religions or Italian food. When I say TREND, I mean MOVEMENT, not fad. When I say TREND, I want you to visualize a mass of humanity surging irrepressibly forward in one primal thrust of desire. And when I say DESIRE, I don't just mean the body trip, but love and marriage and to what purpose? The hottest new thing is nothing but the oldest. People are starting families, having children, no kidding! I am not making this up! You shake your heads, you don't believe it."

We hadn't moved.

"Trust me, kids, we can't afford to be left behind. Sure, there are dolls, surrogates, and whatnot. But Jill, baby, you appear in public with a doll in a stroller and there's no way people aren't going to talk. Inauthenticity won't fly. And I don't mean adoption, either, although there is a place for that and, backs-to-the-wall-wise, we could work that angle. But unselfishness only goes so far, and with the racially mixed thing, you are definitely on thin ice. We don't want to save the world, just sell it baby food. Can't you see it? The beauty is, we don't stop there when there's toys, accessories, preteen designer jeans."

He gasped for breath and waved off the waiter, who couldn't be sure Roger Patterson wasn't choking.

"Don't you think it's worth a try? Don't you think, if I may, the big concern is cost? Most people can't afford the medical bills, schools, clothes, day care, especially when they factor in the sacrifice of time, the loss of personal liberty, the self-denial. Ken and Jill, you are not them. You won't have to change a thing. Do as you please or as you don't please, because we, meaning it, the agency, is going to pay you two dollars for every single dollar you spend on raising a family."

He picked up the check with a bad credit card and when he couldn't make good, I paid. To make amends, he gave me the card to use indefinitely. "A limit problem," he said, "just don't go over fifty."

He dropped us off at the apartment and said to sleep on it, but there was nothing to decide. When we looked at each other that night, it was like we hadn't looked in years.

"Wait a minute, Bucko," said Miriam, "you mean to tell me you didn't fuck?"

"We did but we didn't. You know how it is, being married to Boyd," I said, knowing better than to ask her not to call me Bucko.

"We had an understanding; you had a contract, so why not have kids?"

"They weren't in the contract."

"They weren't not in it."

"Lots of married couples don't have kids, just as lots of them don't get divorced just because they're tired of having sex with each other. We weren't so special. We stayed together for the money, and then they offered us even more money, so it would have been stupid not to try."

"Jeez, wasn't that awful — back to the salt mines."

"It wasn't bad. Sex without birth control. It was like training, except it wasn't drudgery. For the first time in years, we had a goal, but then we kind of fell in love again, so when it turned out we couldn't have kids, we were hurt."

Left to ourselves, Jill and I might not have flopped. The agency didn't operate that way. To increase the likelihood of a multiple birth jackpot, Jill couldn't refuse fertility drugs. The agency kept insisting we would be paid back double, even as they weaseled out of paying thousands of legitimate injury claims, but it didn't occur to us that they wouldn't do what they said they would. We never had more fun screwing the agency.

Roger Patterson tried to sound like he was on our side and not theirs. He might have wanted us to have kids from the start, whether he knew it or not, but he had been too busy making sure we stayed in shape to promote the health club. In our health club promos we had to come across as fit swingers, and in that locker room world, pregnancy wasn't sexy.

Years of birth control made having sex seem to have nothing to do with having kids, which turned out to be how it really was for us. Afterwards, Reno and Seattle posed the kinds of offers you accept if nothing works out. Part of our disappointment was the feeling that having kids was, after all, the least we could do, and we couldn't even do that. Miriam didn't buy any of this and as I went on and on about how it was, I saw her point, but to Jill and me at the time it felt real.

I couldn't get over how hopeful we were. Inside of a couple weeks, Jill started to bloat and everyone thought this was it, as the agency rushed her into a maternity wear deal before the lab could say positive or negative. They signed us up for natural childbirth classes and I did what expectant fathers were supposed to do — not build a crib, but close. I was set up to be one of the new breed of Sensitive Dads, to milk the trend (and to put me to use) so the agency wouldn't think I was worthless. There was an untapped wealth of products for Sensitive Dads, from books to clothes to training courses. I was more convincing as a semi-passive tag-along than as an ex-jock who would rather exercise than turn to fat, and Jill wasn't at all upset by the cameras. Doing her part was never so easy. Unlike the impatient directors of spa commercials, the maternity wear people were cordial.

No session lasted too long. Everyone said she had never looked more radiant. She transformed into the Rose Queen all over again, only without the undercurrents of guilt and fear. On cue she missed a period, so it didn't seem urgent to get medical confirmation, what with our schedule loaded with publicity functions.

Not only that, the agency saw another opportunity. Roger Patterson couldn't get over how Doc-in-a-Box franchise clinics were making a move to supplant traditional forms of health care. Neither family doctor nor hospital emergency room, these places promised the advantages of one without the disadvantages of the other. To tie us in with one of these was irresistible, and it looked like we had a deal. The clinic bolted when they uncovered our health spa reputation.

Meanwhile, the agency landed an endorsement for a do-it-yourself pregnancy test, but Jill's turned up negative. Her doctor confirmed that she wasn't pregnant. The agency accused him of incompetence and tried for a second opinion, which turned out to be that she needed surgery immediately. Needless to say, the maternity wear people had enough of this, as did all of the others.

Some glitch made us responsible for the medical bills, which Roger Patterson paid without telling us. When she found out, Jill felt irredeemably ashamed of all the bad stuff she had ever said about her father.

After that, nothing was the same. And rather than begin the long, slow countdown to divorce, maybe we should have split up then, but a Sensitive Non-Dad doesn't leave his wife in the wake of her hysterectomy.

Miriam and I didn't want to stay in Colorado any more than Jill and I had after her operation. All around us were people whose lives weren't going down the drain. Blame it on the mountain air, but this wasn't a place where you could get away with not working. It wasn't the tropics. It wasn't a city full of things to watch. Compared to Omaha, Oklahoma City, and Fort Worth, though, it wasn't far behind San Francisco.

Entering territory burned up by my health club days, I shouldn't have passed judgment on any place or anything, but we would have been better off heading straight for New Orleans.

"I don't want to go to New Orleans," she said.

"Why not? It's not Mardi Gras or the Sugar Bowl. There's nothing happening that we ought to avoid."

She wouldn't say. It wasn't because she had lived there. I had lived there, so it shouldn't have been up to her to turn it down.

"I didn't veto Reno and Denver and I didn't like living in those places. New Orleans, though, wasn't bad. Why can't you do New Orleans?"

"I just don't want to go. If you're lucky, you'll never find out why."

Arguing did no good. I couldn't say that New Orleans was everything that Denver wasn't. All around us, the busy, strong, hard-working, willful people went through their routines, and as we stood in line at the supermarket you couldn't have told me that this wasn't Utah. No one had less than three pounds of hamburger, which got Miriam sneering about cow towns. She wouldn't keep her voice down, so I tried to calm her by saying that snow was to blame. The threat of inevitable snow drove people to assume a bunker mentality. They could not put off what had to be done to prepare for winter. This wasn't unrealistic, I said, but what I wanted to say was that if we couldn't go to New Orleans or California or Mexico, we might as well spend the rest of the trip in cow towns, where all there was to save us from bland food was food made by Mexicans, which wasn't as good and cheap as what you could eat where they didn't cater to tastes spoiled by hamburgers.

We weren't out of the store two seconds before a man with a camera came up to us. Neither of us should have wanted to stop, yet we needed some kind of diversion. To begin with, he didn't look like the others. He was small with dark and oily hair, and as he slinked around the pudgy blond burger people, nobody else would give him a tumble.

Not that they were rude. The question was the problem, which he wouldn't have admitted if he hadn't been here all afternoon. What would it take to buy your soul? and What's your least favorite TV show? and If you could get away with murder, who would you kill? had needed no more than an hour to fill the space. In the past, he had made up the question, but this one came from his editor because his editor said the Inquiring Photographer column was not a sandbox where sick minds played.

"We pay nothing but your picture in the paper and your words in print," he said.

"We don't care," said Miriam, "shoot."

"What was," his tone went into inquisitor overdrive, daring you not to come clean, "your greatest accomplishment?"

Miriam didn't hesitate. She told him about a trick she played on Wolfie at the Mirror Lounge – not all of it, but more than they would publish. This wasn't as extreme as what she had done to Boyd, but the Inquiring Photographer ate it up. He said she understood "greatest" to mean having the most impact — not necessarily to be something you were proud of having done.

"Who says I'm not proud of it?"

Shopping carts skittered around me under a fierce bright sky as he snapped what couldn't fail to be a perfect photo. Even if he didn't believe me, many would see the picture and remember. He only had to check the paper's files, although the sports pages of the early seventies wouldn't have as many as the scandal sheets a few years later.

I didn't answer, but reached into my shirt. He didn't relax when I pulled it out.

"That's a gold medal, isn't it? You don't look like an — I mean, it must have been a while ago."

The shopping carts stopped and the crowd closed in and suddenly I realized that no law says you have to tell the truth to a stranger who asks personal questions in a parking lot, especially if he's a reporter.

"He thought I had a flush," I said, "that it was safe to bet all he had on a full house, but it wasn't just a flush."

The crowd grumbled and the photographer asked if I wasn't a professional gambler.

"No, I'm unemployed."

"And your greatest accomplishment was winning a gold medal in a poker game," he unloaded.

"You didn't let me finish. I didn't want the medal, but he didn't have a car. I told him he could buy it back later, that the medal was no more than a marker, an I.O.U. He wouldn't go for that."

"So, the greatest deed you ever did was give an American gold medallist a chance to buy back what nothing could replace?"

"No, I refused his wife. Not that she wasn't beautiful or that she wouldn't have been worth it. It wouldn't have been right."

"Don't be like that, Chick, tell him the truth."

He looked from me to Miriam as the shopping carts

scuttled away, so why not? I told him the truth and said I was sorry and he thanked me and said he thought there was something familiar about me, but the next day the paper unmasked me as a card sharp whose greatest accomplishment was trading an Olympian's gold medal back to him for a night with his wife.

We didn't have until sundown to leave town.

Jill and I arrived in Denver in midsummer, when no day didn't hit ninety. All we knew of Colorado prepared us for Boulder, not a mile-high version of Phoenix. Smog hid the mountains and we were stranded on the wrong side of them, in a desert of apartments, shopping centers, tract houses, and no buildings that hadn't gone up recently. The agency joked that Denver wasn't hell so much as Purgatory.

Although they put us where a couple could blend in, this was undoubtedly a singles ghetto. Not a weekend went by without some kind of get-together. Since many of the tenants were lawyers and marketing directors, if not sports fans, they might have known who I was. They didn't say. The agency advised us like Perry Mason telling a client about to be picked up for murder: register in a strange place under our real names, as if nothing could have been more normal than for us to move here.

Nobody cared. They were too into themselves to bother with us, and even when one of them cruised in our direction, it wasn't for who we were.

Before the agency asked us to breed, it was tempting to pretend we weren't married. Jill didn't look over twenty-two, and my swimming muscles hadn't completely degenerated. With some changing partners eight nights a week, a come-on wasn't much different from belonging to a book club: if you don't send it back, it's yours.

Not for morality as much as image, our contract had a morals clause. There was something to say for having America's Couple not get caught pants-down. The agency made it plain they didn't care what we did, as long as they didn't find out. This was nothing but a dare.

Together or apart, Jill and I couldn't resist the lure of the pool. The women and men were abnormally attractive. You couldn't have complained about waking up next to anybody of the opposite sex, unless you wanted somebody of the same sex, which wasn't rare. Being unemployed meant I spent time at the pool. It must have seemed as if I wasn't there just for a tan.

I didn't like sun, and swimming pools made me edgy. There was little to do besides pretend to read, which others did as if they weren't cruising. It was okay to talk, as long as you kept it meaningless. The agency had said not to talk about the past; they didn't have to tell me not to swim. The smell of chlorine was repulsive, unveiled by the sight of that fake blue fluid wobbling inside its tile frame. Swimming pools meant getting up out of a warm bed in the dark to go through the cold to a room filled with chemicals to dive churning relentlessly into the taste and the temperature of blood.

And yet, not only the pretty women in bathing suits made me return to the scene of misery. The health club demonstrations should have cured me of any pride, but there was no denying that I liked to win or forgetting that I had won. Not only that, I could beat anyone here.

Spending hours by the pool, you got to know people in ways that have nothing to do with talking. At the shopping centers you might run into someone and nod, even though you weren't sure how you knew her, until later, when you saw her without her clothes on. And when it came to poolside conversation, it was strange how the people most willing to talk were the ones who came prepared not to talk because they came to the pool with books, which were no more than props.

"I haven't read that one, but I heard it's outrageous," she said.

"It can't be as good as yours."

They say don't judge a book by its cover, but hers was a brighter foil. The edges of her pages were brilliant green while mine were a nondescript white. We bought them off the racks at convenience stores that told you where they stood on the bestseller list, but you couldn't buy just any book. Some weren't for men, others weren't for women. Books not for men were written by women and had covers with women men wanted. Books not for women were written by men and had covers with men or submarines. Exceptions made it hard to choose without looking inside.

We introduced ourselves to each other but didn't shake hands. She was lying on her front with her back undone. For all that people around here shared and showed, women at the pool weren't allowed to bare their nipples.

Her name was Margaret and I had seen her with about six different guys, which was neither unusual nor obvious. You knew what she did with them, but you didn't know, unless you were one of them.

"I hear you're a jock," she said, and I wasn't surprised. My cover story had made the rounds, so I didn't have to tell everyone that a stress fracture ruined my dream to go for The Ironman.

She knew about triathlons and she had been to Hawaii when they held The Ironman, so it wouldn't do to keep talking about sports.

"You haven't told me what you are," I said.

"Stewardess — no, flight attendant."

"Don't you want to go for navigator?"

"I've done worse," she said, uncapping the lotion for me to smear her back.

Finally, she said, "Kenny, you're an unusual man. I'm having a party tonight, if you've got nothing on. I haven't met your wife. Bring her, why don't you?"

It couldn't have been more innocent, but Jill didn't want to go. Her father's business had made our social life part of the job, so she never missed an opportunity to miss a party. Not me. After months of virtual house arrest, nothing could keep me from going out.

I knew better than to be on time, but coming late meant you couldn't go home early. At 8:30 I knocked on the only door in the corridor that had no music pounding from the other side.

"Your wife couldn't make it," said a guy who called himself Bill.

"No, she's sick," I said, thinking ill/ pill/ Jill/ Bill so I wouldn't forget his name.

Bill looked familiar, but not from the pool. It shouldn't have mattered that I couldn't place him, unless he worked for the agency. If he did, we couldn't say, since Margaret wasn't supposed to know. Or maybe this is just some notion I'd picked up from the books that weren't for women.

Nobody else was here, except for Margaret.

"Bottoms up," she handed me a Margarita glowing the color of a sleeveless dress that made her seem browner than she was.

"How do you like my view?" she couldn't have been serious. In every direction from her balcony there was nothing but flat roads, fast-food stands, shopping centers, and Monopoly game houses with enormous antennas.

"Bill, we don't have enough ice. Wouldn't you know

— Margaritas are so demanding."

Bill said it was no trouble, but he slammed the door with the sound that made me feel sealed inside a pressurized chamber.

"Nothing but boys," she said.

"He's not your — "

"He nobody, just a friend."

"What's he do?" I said, as if it wasn't irrelevant.

"What does anyone do, and isn't it all the same?"

"Not exactly," I put down my glass.

When she bent to refill it, I saw she wore no bra. That wasn't all. Bill hadn't gone out for ice: he had gone. No more guests would come. This was right out of the books, whether they weren't for women or men. My stewardess flight attendant had to be an agent, working for the agency to render my contract null and void.

Jill and I hadn't been in town long and the fallout from the spas was unending. This was before they hatched the family plan, which wouldn't have been necessary if they could have cut me loose on a morals violation. Implausible? When Roger Patterson popped the breeding question, the idea that they would have to put me through such a test wasn't so implausible.

Trapped in the singles pad of a gorgeous playgirl, I couldn't diddle with scenarios. Her lips were wet and my mouth was dry, but even a marriage that had run aground on my suspicion of Jill masturbating to *The Diary of Anaïs Nin* couldn't persuade me that one night of good sex would be worth losing a lousy paycheck.

"It won't work," I said.

"Don't you want to let me fix it? You wouldn't believe how good I am with tools."

"No hard feelings, you have a job to do, so do I. Thanks for the drink and I wish I didn't have to go, but if it's any consolation, when I'm with her, I'll think of you." I nodded good-bye as she shook her head in recognition and disbelief.

-3

The agency used to refer carelessly to the five year plan, making the health club sound like a communist development project instead of a scam. Those in charge had a misplaced sense of trust. They devised a system that was supposed to grow from cooperation, even though the people apt to be recruited to manage the branches weren't the sort to cooperate. Not that the underlings were less greedy than the overseers, just unencumbered by dignity. Much as the agency tried to study the health club field, their research of the operation of a single spa didn't translate to the operation of a chain of spas. But Roger Patterson had made a career out of launching successful franchises, so the agency figured his expertise couldn't fail to make the chain catch fire. After the five years it took for Gold Medal Health Spas to be dismantled by lawsuits, some of the middlemen escaped with small fortunes, as the expansion drive encouraged the affiliates to run wild.

In 1973, there couldn't have been a better place for us to incorporate than Booth, Oklahoma; in 1978, the central headquarters had to be sold to the neighborhood televangelist. The Reverend Jimmy Ray held telethon baptisms in the pool where I'd done my demos, until the feds caught up with him and forced him to divest and pay taxes because they claimed his church was illegitimate. Some weren't as angry as others at throwing all of their money away, and so groups of followers attacked one another. A faction that called themselves The Infidels torched the office and the reverend's mansion. It was a miracle that nobody died.

Although some said the reverend resented us for moving into his territory, we never had any trouble with him. If anything, we brought each other more customers, and the town had to like having two non-polluting local industries. Any conflict would have been over image, which in our enterprise wasn't a negligible thing. Jimmy Ray and Pearl had to be King and Queen, though, so when America's Couple moved in, they couldn't have been overjoyed. They weren't as glamorous as we were, yet they couldn't attack us because I was a national hero and our message was good, clean health. We never said anything bad about them. When the subject of Jimmy Ray came up, the agency told us to say no more than, "Jimmy Ray, I like him, he's good people." We couldn't alienate him and we couldn't support him. We became the kind of neighbor everyone should have: one who doesn't mess with you.

Not that we had time for a social life. It may have looked like smiles and flexes, but the exercise business was unflinching exercise. It wasn't real exercise for us, though, because our job was just to look good going through the motions. Jill would stretch some and I'd do no more than a lap in the pool and then the instructors took over. The hardest part was not eating too much.

The agency didn't want us to get involved with the office, which was a mistake. We would travel to branch spas whose managers were surprised we hadn't come to check up on them. Rather than ask questions, we posed for pictures, so word couldn't help getting around. Toward the end, they didn't bother to hide what they did.

A big selling point for Gold Medal Health Spas was the Tone-o-matic, which let customers ("clients") do nothing while they got whipped into shape. These weren't exercise machines but glorified vibrators, not much different from the magic fingers of a motel bed. They cost plenty because they had to look like they weren't nothing, but they weren't nearly as expensive as the branch managers said they were. A complicated set of instructions nobody read contained adjustments that would have made them cost-effective, if there hadn't been more money to be made by embezzling the repair fund than by doing routine maintenance on the machines.

This scam would have gone on indefinitely had the customers not begun to get hurt. It didn't stop at nagging backache. Ruptured discs weren't uncommon. The lawsuits were incredible and unbeatable. Nobody settled out of court, but if a few had settled before the company went under, at least they could have got some gain for their pain.

The court ordered the machines destroyed, yet when Miriam and I went through the ruins of the ex-center and desanctified video church, there it was on the altar: an aluminum sacrifice.

Why hadn't Miriam and I expected Booth to be deserted? With the reverend locked up, the health club long gone, and the nearest solvent bank no nearer than a distant memory, the service businesses couldn't continue trading with each other. Somewhere in the past there had been cattle drives, and there once was a rumor of silver, but ranching and mining never really got off the ground. The land wasn't worthless, though, and there was hope during the fifties that the Air Force would move here. They didn't even sink a missile silo. Too far off the trail to be a wayside stopover and too far removed from all of the hopes and dreams that ever put it in action in the first place, Booth nevertheless had the look of a town under the protection of some kind of caretaker. Eventually we saw why: a billboard put up by none other than the agency advised producers to contact them for film rights.

Other signs said NO TRESPASSING. And all the mattresses probably still had their Do-not-remove-this-tag-under-penalty-of-law tags.

"Oh boy, this is like the Twilight Zone after a nuclear war," said Miriam, as if nothing could have pleased her more.

"No it isn't. We can't stay."

"Who says we can't?"

"We can but we can't. Not forever."

"Never forever, just until we run out of food."

"Or until somebody comes," I said, pointing to the graffiti and beer cans, the piss patches and tire stains that left no doubt what teenagers did for fun.

"We can hide, can't we?"

It wasn't smart to stay in a ghost town indefinitely. We couldn't be the only ones who wanted a row of deserted buildings to ourselves. And yet, we didn't head straight for the saloon. We parked among the ditched junkers that looked no different from our car, and made the rounds.

Booth had more past than present, and a negative future. It didn't look Old West as much as 1955. Not that it couldn't have been made to look older. Things weren't squared so much as rounded, like a model train village I used to have. In one of the garages that could have been a barn were stacks of fake cornices and railings and unlabeled crates that had been broken open, so anyone could see the contents weren't worth stealing.

When I lived here, people bragged about not locking doors. That hadn't changed. Off the highway, two side streets went nowhere. We knocked and entered each of the two dozen houses, and hardly a cupboard didn't have food, while some had more than I hoped we would want. You couldn't blame them for not taking the beans and cocoa, the orange crystals, creamed corn, and dregs of spices, but one house had crabmeat and another had pint bottles of vodka stashed everywhere.

Miriam peeled off her jeans in no time when she found a wedding dress that had been dyed black.

"Why be in the dollhouse if you can't be the doll?" she said.

None of the men's clothes fit me in this town with men who were a little too skinny or much too fat, but when Miriam put on a dress, she made it hers.

We couldn't resist checking every room of every house. The more we collected, the less I wanted, and yet there was something about the opportunity to plunder that made the act of plundering irresistible. What if these things weren't cast-offs but props? The scenes of disorder could have been staged, so that by removing anything, we ruined a set designed for a movie to be shot next week. If not props, maybe these knick-knacks were for film crews to play with when they got bored.

After the houses, we couldn't resist the shops. These were more topsy-turvy than the rooms where people had lived, as if the vandals thought private places weren't public enough to showcase what they could do. In the seventies, the clothing store, food market, gun shop, and even the bank weren't where you would expect to see drawings of blow jobs all over the walls. The drawings were only face and cock, and although they were more or less realistic, the faces didn't look like the famous actresses the captions said they were.

It was hard to tell at a glance which shop was which, and I couldn't remember. Broken wood, bent glass, burnt cans, and a foot-deep litter of shotgun shells and blown fireworks kept us guessing, but didn't make us dig. One thing we didn't find was any kind of rubber, but these weren't places to come for safe sex.

When we reached the center of the defunct spa empire, there seemed to be nothing to salvage. Fires had a way of making trash worse than garbage, yet even without hope of finding treasure, we had to explore. The smell of melted plastic hung in the air and the walls were no longer the orange the agency painted them or the white the reverend plastered them or even black from flames, but a tangle of cables and wires and fluff. There were no walls, only drapes of what normally went between surfaces. Wires, pipes, and insulation were welded into an unbreakable gunk. It would have been a cave, except everywhere glowed because there was no roof.

With the nearest hospital too far away, we shouldn't have walked around in here. We weren't the kind of people to get kicks from flirting with danger, and even simple caution took more effort than we were used to. In here, you didn't dare take a step without holding back your weight, until it was certain there was something underneath. Then the air changed and the floor dropped, signaling that we had crossed a threshold, and while everything lay covered by a smooth gray ash, we didn't trust the shine.

"No, wait," Miriam stopped me.

She was right: vodka wasn't as sensible as beans. Not that it mattered what I threw, the can plunged, sending thick waves to the edges and corners and back again, uncorking a stink worse than corpses.

"Not there," I said before she stepped, "it's bigger than you think: Olympic-sized."

The health club rules were still posted, but then the prohibitions of swimming pools couldn't be much different from those of baptisteries.

"No cannonballs!"

"Nothing but serious swimming," I said.

"No wonder it went down the toilet."

As the scum settled, we picked our way around to an area that had been but wasn't a locker room. The video church had apparently combined this with what we called "the machine shop" to make the main sanctuary, which was an easy conversion, since the agency had trolleys for overhead lights in order to feature shots of clients undressing in the commercials. The smashed lights didn't look like they'd stay up a moment longer, but at least by being here they showed we were actually where I thought we were.

The other props were nothing we had used them for. Not only were our benches their pews, our starting blocks their pulpit, and our mirrors their stained glass, they had used our Tone-o-matic for their altar. It wasn't the sacrifice after all.

"Go for the gold!" I shot off swimming through a few feet of videotape, not knowing why they used my real voice. It wasn't the Chipmunks, but was far from Charlton Heston. Maybe they were after a breathless excitement, vigor, pep. Looking back, I see how Jack La Lanne and Richard Simmons had voices to coax people off the couch, while mine sounded no better than a tin plate parody of theirs. At the time, nobody noticed as much as kids. At swimming pools all over the country, a kid would scream, "Go for the gold!" and take off like a maniac, and even if he wasn't mocking me, he was.

You couldn't watch a morning movie or late night re-run without seeing us. The ads opened with a shot of Jill in a leotard, stretching and gasping to leave no doubt what exercise was good for. A voice-over went, "You don't have to be an Olympic champion to hit the floor and ask for more," or, "Take the chance and do the dance," or, "Do the thing that makes her sing," while disco music beat out a montage of skin-tight women and throbbing men. The ads weren't ahead of their time. Neither did they look like they cost too much to make. The address and phone number flashed on the screen while the announcer said in one-two exercise cadence, "Don't delay, and act today."

You wouldn't think such a pitch would attract anyone, but Gold Medal Health Spas went from nowhere to *the* place to be, overnight. And yet, not until the next decade did enough people of a certain age have the money to finance the image of themselves as sexy.

In those days, we lived in nothing but sweatsuits, except when I stripped to swim or Jill to stretch or Roger Patterson to show off.

"Never felt better," he said. "Not the rubdowns and the machines, but sweat is where it's at."

Like other media mavens, he had a shameless knack for appropriating lines from songs and protest marches that only a few years earlier had attacked everything he stood for. This, along with his habit of butting in on the demonstrations, while discouraging us from learning about the business, might have annoyed us if he hadn't been so ridiculous. As a joke, we gave him a U.S.

Olympic Team warm-up jacket; he went nowhere without it and made us call him Coach. That way, he didn't look strange when he went up to a woman and grabbed her thighs.

Roger Patterson wasn't a total nitwit. "Heart rate, heart rate, that's it, do it to it, no mercy, no mercy," he'd say before anyone might belt him, peppering his line with gym jargon.

If Jill's stepmother complained, he'd take a business trip to another spa, so mostly she said nothing and only minded the till. Afterwards, nobody begrudged Belinda the $300,000 she ran off with because she had earned a lot more. Besides, if she hadn't taken it, the lawyers would have.

Belinda kept her original name, Mathews, and didn't wear work-out clothes or work out. She didn't need to: in jeans, she had a body that could sell memberships. Her secret was not to eat stupidly, which didn't mean you had to guzzle vegetable juice and gobble vitamins but to avoid most of what you thought tasted good. She was a native Californian, an ex-model who had married and come east to Oklahoma to slow down from a life that had gone too fast: not an Okie but a cokie. She didn't blame Roger Patterson that the health club circuit was more hectic than Hollywood.

"I'm no babe in the woods. You'd think I didn't have a clue, but appearances deceive. I wasn't a model for twenty years for nothing. So kid, you can listen to what I have to say or you can not listen, but you've got to get a hold of yourself and make the shot."

Jill sobbed head-in-arms after another demonstration where the director yelled at her while Belinda paced, snapping a fly swatter not just for effect.

"I hate this place, there's nothing to do, we just get two channels."

"Look," said Belinda, "it's a fact of life that men have no brains where their balls are. Not that we should want to rearrange that, but they like looking at us. It's not a disadvantage."

Belinda wasn't a cupcake. She enjoyed reading and thinking, so she seemed unusual. We admired her for this, and for the casual, uninvolved way she ran the spa.

"There's a public self and a private self," Belinda went on as she massaged Jill's back, "but it isn't enough to limit the split to one and the selves to two."

She had a way of talking that wasn't too fast or too slow, so the words came out easily and not in a rush. She may not have been all that old and wise, but she made us feel stupid for being so young.

When nobody else would go outside, the three of us went on picnics. It would be high noon in July, a hundred in the sun because there was no shade. We packed hot coffee and dried fruit and no sandwiches. We took the car in order to go where we could see nothing different from what the Indians saw, assuming the Indians saw old washing machines, beer cans, and power lines.

"Sometimes I miss Santa Monica," said Jill, "that pier with the shabby little shops, the roller skating, the water, or no, the beach."

"The beach is nothing but false poetry," said Belinda.

Jill wouldn't stop.

"There wasn't anything we couldn't do. Our way was the freeway, and you didn't have to get off at Pasadena when you thought, hey, why not Palm Springs? But you know, sometimes I wish we had kept going, that I'd never been in that parade."

Belinda said, "There are two kinds of California Girl, those who wanted to be and those who never wanted to be Rose Queen, but there are just a few who can say never for sure."

"Sorry," said Jill, "I didn't mean — "

"I can't complain, I made the most of my day in the sun."

Hadn't we made the most of ours? Some ex-Rose Queens and ex-Olympians gave up the life in order to take real jobs and start families, while others rode their floats in porno movies or put their shots in bars. We had nothing to apologize for. It wasn't our fault that we were born to be put on a pedestal. That didn't mean we had no problems. If we couldn't talk to Belinda, why be her friend? Except she wasn't a friend, she was a stepmother. And she had her own problems, so we couldn't just talk: we had to listen.

"We said we were actresses, and they said they would make us stars, so nobody had to lie for sex or drugs any more than a fish had to pretend to swim. If the rivers dried, there was always Vegas, because nobody cared what you did as long as you made the shot or what you shot as long as you left no tracks. By the week we sold dream houses we tore down on weekends, in scenes nightmares couldn't imagine. We were the picture perfect wives, holding up soap and opening freezers and smiling in front of vacuum cleaners, yet never forgetting to flirt with anyone who could make us actresses for real."

"It couldn't have been that bad," said Jill.

"Not bad: fantastic."

"It's not the same," I told Miriam.

Kneeling at the Tone-o-matic altar, I saw what hadn't been there before: straps and electrodes.

"At least there's no juice," she said when the switch

didn't work. "You don't think they put people in that contraption."

"Religion's not my strong suit, but the gist behind this looks more Spanish Inquisition than First-Born Son."

"No wonder they trashed the place."

"Maybe it wasn't the reverend. Maybe it was for a commercial," I said, as if it couldn't be real.

If the same crowd that came here on motorcycles did the overhaul, I didn't want to be around when they came back. Reinforced cable went from the machine toward the back-up power source, because out here you couldn't live without a generator. Miriam followed me through the fluff hung like Georgia moss in the cold sun of Oklahoma until we swiped to where the smell of burn plastic gave way to the smell of oil, not tar but a sweetness like 3-in-1. There was the generator, the beer cans, the unfinished jug of some red fuel: Red Rooster 21, Wine of the 21st Century.

"What if it's not wine?" I said.

"Of course it's not wine. We will serve no wine before it's time for you to buy me a drink."

Ads for defunct beer came out of the dust of the saloon, above shelves that weren't empty, even if the bottles were. Instead of green felt tables, there were booths with red vinyl and black Formica, and through it all came the oddly unreflected gleam of chrome stool pipe legs. There wasn't a piano and no heads hung on the walls. Among the signs were paintings of cowboys and Indians doing things to each other that could have been sex and not violence. Brown crust coated the bowls next to beers that had evaporated to fossilized layers, but you couldn't count the rings for years. Behind the bar was a bayonet: no match for a gun. Kegs were hooked up, and when you pulled the tap, a sewage spluttered bubbles that made you wish you hadn't pulled.

"In heaven there ain't no beer," said Miriam.

Without water, we couldn't stay, but the faucet spat brown, then orange, then yellow cleaner than the iron fresh from any well.

"At least we have vodka," I said, finding small and narrow glasses that didn't hold as much as you thought they did.

Although it was supposed to taste like nothing, I thought vodka tasted like puking raw potato after siphoning gasoline.

"Come on, Chick, not straight when there's mixer."

"You can't be serious."

"Reasonably fresh pineapple, you with me or not?"

"Drink through the rust and you won't see the morning."

"Check for more — they can't all be fucked."

They weren't but they were. None of the cans looked safe, until we got to prunes, except they weren't prunes.

"Who wouldn't rather have olives than vermouth?" I said.

It didn't take long to get the wood stove going, and for light there were lanterns.

"Didn't you used to hang out here, Chick?"

"Nothing else to do."

"That must have been nice, wasn't it? Hanging out at the town bar, no matter how different you all were?"

"It wasn't just a bar. There was nowhere else in town to sit and eat, except at the Busy Bee, and the Busy Bee wasn't open at night. If we didn't feel like health food, we ate here. Not that the food was better than the stuff at the Carrot Cafe."

In fact, none of it came close to crabmeat and olives, just as none of their martinis were as good as these.

There was no sign of a name, although there had been a name, The Corral or The Ricochet Room, but everyone called it Jepson's.

"We'd come here and talk about places we'd rather be that were nowhere near here, like New York or San Francisco. We talked like we were missing something, not being able to go to bars that had more than two kinds of Scotch. Then, in those towns, we never found any hangouts as good as this."

"Jill didn't mind this place, huh Chick?"

"You're not kidding! We even — no, I can't."

"Can't what?"

"Danced, although we didn't know how, and everyone stared."

"Aw, that's sweet," said Miriam, but she wasn't teasing. "Tell you what, let's dance, music or not."

"No, I forget."

"Nobody's looking and you never knew how, anyhow."

"We couldn't do the Texas 2-step and we couldn't swing. We weren't drunk or bored, but there was something about that music that made it hard to sit still. Even the slow songs got to you, songs you thought you couldn't stand after hearing them half a dozen times a night."

Miriam wasn't Patsy Cline, but when she sang she wasn't exactly Miriam, either. She pulled me to her and we started what wasn't a dance so much as a moving hug. The lace of her dress pressed through the cotton of my shirt, and we looked at each other without looking away. Wood crackled in the stove and shadows from the flames bounced off the walls and it hit me that there was nothing about this moment I'd ever want to forget. The smell of our unwashed hair, the cigarette smoke, and the taste of olives stripped by alcohol; every smudge and line in the background setting off her face, my face, her voice and the way she looked at me, nipple to nipple and crotch to crotch, I tried to feel how it felt because this is what I wanted to remember the moment that I died.

Ours wasn't the first health club chain, but the agency had a plan to make us seem revolutionary. Instead of opening in cities, where the customers were, we popped up all over the country, in places the customers didn't live and so had to reach by a kind of pilgrimage. There was a spiel about blending the physical with the spiritual, which came down to charging extra for room and board in rates that said Grand Hotel for accommodations that said Boot Camp, because this wasn't a dude ranch. People had to commit themselves to the program or they wouldn't succeed, so the worse they were treated, the better they liked it.

Not that they lived in a barracks. No matter how many cells were crammed into the space, people had their own rooms. They weren't allowed to smoke, drink, or eat the wrong food, stay up past curfew or sleep late, hang out in town or roam the plains. That left one thing, except the beds weren't big enough for two.

The Carrot Cafe didn't stay open past ten. Its sauna heat made everyone strip while Belinda served juices laced with vitamins and Roger made the rounds, towel around his neck, and if asked, I wasn't to deny that he knew "the way." Jill and I never stayed long in the cafe. Our cell was a twelve-room ranch house, so we didn't need this for a living room. The agency wanted us to make appearances for appearance's sake, just as it wanted us not to stay, for the same reason, so Roger Patterson worked the crowd, Belinda served them, and we smiled.

At least the agency didn't care what we did outside of this, as long as we didn't get too chummy with the reverend. The reverend and Pearl didn't look or talk like us, but they, too, were stuck in a routine that never ended. Jimmy Ray went after the poor and uneducated, who'd send in their savings so they wouldn't go to hell — not the young with good jobs, who'd give out their credit cards in order to dream that they would live forever. We both thrived on the suspension of disbelief. His followers, like ours, were happy to think how different they were from other followers, and from the way we told jokes about the rollers, I figured they didn't hold back the jokes about us.

If there was any justification for letting myself get swept along by the agency, it came from thinking that, had I been in control, I still couldn't have acted on my own. This gig was no different from Jimmy Ray's, in a way. Every smile, wave, and stroke, every leg lift and bead of sweat was for the benefit of an imagined audience, and for all of the freedom Jill or I thought we had, we couldn't deviate from what this public thought we should be. In other words, we couldn't smoke cigarettes any more than Jimmy Ray and Pearl could tout Camus.

In the media game, you could reverse yourself, as long as you didn't botch the recovery. For a preacher, nothing went over bigger than confessing to sin, the gaudier the better. He could kill and later say it wasn't his fault, even though Flip Wilson's signature line, "The devil made me do it," had gone from stand-up to Hallmark. For that matter, the agency could have made us start smoking in order to launch a campaign to make us stop, providing their tobacco company client didn't object.

The glamour of syndicated TV stardom came down to a shtick that made me almost wish I worked on an assembly line, where the rule of monotony made any exception an unexpected pleasure, and where there was hope that the same thing wouldn't keep happening. One day it didn't.

"Don't be mad at me," said Jill.

I didn't know what she meant because I couldn't remember ever being mad at her.

"There was no getting around it, I had to accept, but if you want, we can cancel."

She ran into Pearl at the Busy Bee, and because they couldn't help recognizing each other, they said hello.

"Well honey, y'all enjoying our town?" Pearl said in a way that didn't seem unfriendly.

"Yes, mmh, uhh," Jill bit the egg, and when she showed me how nervous she'd been, I couldn't help feeling sorry for her. "I do miss home, though," she went on, unconsciously mimicking the woman who was only trying to make her feel comfortable.

"Ain't nobody from Booth, Oklahoma, hon, we all must pass through."

Jill said she had a high, silky voice, and that it wouldn't hurt to go to dinner.

We took off our sweats and put on our dress clothes, nothing fancy but nothing sloppy because it had to be carefully picked. Their house wasn't far, but we didn't want to arrive on foot. We couldn't bring wine, but had to bring something. Jill carried flowers, but from me no ordinary gift would do: it had to be a relic of my victory. "An Olympian's triumph is not his alone," had been drummed into us. Enough people bought it, so it couldn't be ignored. I never got over how people went for the fake medals, old sweatshirts, used earplugs, and bathing caps.

"You shouldn't have," said the reverend, lifting it out of the wrapper. "Not a bathing cap for Bullwinkle. No, underpants for a bed wetter!"

Ordinarily, the tank suit wasn't a flop, but the reverend might have put down any souvenir.

"Jimmy Ray, don't be like that," said Pearl. "Thank the boy for his unselfish offering."

"And to think I couldn't go a night without soaking the mattress. I can't thank you enough."

"Don't pay him no mind," said Pearl. "Truth is, he can't wait to stuff himself into that cute little thing and prance afore the mirror."

Nobody was supposed to take these things for what they had been, but for what they could be. Yesterday's tank suits were today's trophies and tomorrow's trade, I didn't say, not bothering to add that you could raise a lot of money for a video church by auctioning off crap like this on the air.

"Let's go to the pool room," the reverend wrapped an arm around me so I couldn't get away.

"I have no servants," Pearl was saying to Jill, "because I believe in doing everything myself, but you can help."

Jimmy Ray led me downstairs and made the green glow with a snap of the overhead, spreading the table from the edges of darkness to a revelation of a pinball machine called Beat the Devil, with angel wings for flippers, cherub bumpers, and a scoreboard in the clouds above the inevitable downward slope to send balls to hell.

"I don't play anymore," said the reverend. "It's no fun when you own the machine. Not like pool."

When he offered a game of 500 to start, I thought he wanted to play straight pool to 500, but he meant dollars, not points. I said I hadn't brought any money, and he said he knew I was good for it. I said I hadn't played in years, and he said we could play nine ball, where anyone could win by luck, off the break.

"O.K., but let's play for nothing."

"500 ain't nothing," said the reverend, racking the diamond set, "but I can't be a bad host."

He made drinks that didn't look like bourbon so much as Coke, even if they were dark rum and ice. I won three out of four, proving that skill was irrelevant.

"I can't play for nothing," he said. "Let's play for appearances: if you win, I can't refuse to be on your show."

"What if I don't want you on my show?"

"Then lose, and you'll be on mine, testifying like never before."

"Anyway, I don't have a show. We just tape commercials, or I walk around preaching that you shouldn't stop exercising."

"You don't think I could sell a few memberships?"

I didn't care, but the reverend had another deal.

"If you win, I and all of my disciples shall prostrate myself before you, pay for the course, and join in exercise, while if I win, you shall not be obliged to join the church."

"Not heads I win, tails you lose?"

"You can't lose, but if you do, then you agree to give my camera free roam in search of iniquity. Fifteen minutes is all I need to send the eyes of retribution throughout the sin-ridden catacombs of your Vatican, that I might unveil it to expose the latter-day Gomorrah."

"You can have that for nothing, any time. I don't care what you do with your camera, but I'm not authorized to make deals. I'm nothing but a model. I could recommend you to the agency, but I have no clout. If anything, I'm a negative influence."

He dropped it and we went upstairs to a dinner of fried chicken, cole slaw, biscuits, and iced tea, except ours wasn't tea.

"Not bad," I said, although it wasn't any better than the stuff from the national chain.

Pearl ate like there was no dessert. She grunted and smacked and gasped from the moment the reverend finished saying grace to well past the time everyone else finished, but then people who spend two hours a day on live TV begging like pious baboons shouldn't have to act unnatural off camera. The reverend didn't talk business at the table. He asked Jill about us, all of the stuff we never thought about because it hadn't happened very long ago.

"It wasn't long after Munich," said Jill. "I didn't exactly work for the agency. Daddy didn't know what to do with me, so they put me in the New York office while they tried to decide. I was there to learn, and then when Kenny walked in, they couldn't have set it up any better. Daddy and Kenny's dad worked out a contract, and I took him to lunch, and while it wasn't for more than an endorsement at first, we started going out to dinner."

We weren't together two weeks before Spitz signed with a rival agency. He was way ahead of me, in medals and endorsements, but the agency said not to worry, that he'd only make it easier. From way before the Olympics, they had lined up all sorts of promos for whatever gold medal swimmer they landed, including but not limited to jockwear, waterproof accessories, and one of those ersatz postseason college football games in a Florida town trying to leap off the map and onto TV.

At the beginning, it was strictly a solo spot, without Jill. Although there was talk about pairing me in a few quick hitters with a woman winner, they mostly wanted someone more or less anonymous, whose identity could be revised to suit the product.

I couldn't care less. I was twenty-one, and could order anything off of any menu because never again would I have to get up at five AM to swim.

We weren't the only two people in the city, but with

all of the deals, negotiations, and appearances, it was hard for us not to talk to each other like we were. We couldn't do anything for ourselves. Rides, meals, hotels, what to wear or not to wear were all calls made by the agency. Not that we had a lot to do. Everything depended on Spitz, or on the market, or on what seemed to be the coming trend, so it was better not to get too hopeful. If I'd been the star of the Olympics, the agency wouldn't have hesitated, but they aimed to maneuver for the long haul.

"Kenny didn't have to propose and I didn't have to accept – we knew! It was on a ride in Central Park or dinner at the Top of the Sixes or – no, I'm confusing it with a promo. I mean, it wasn't something people did. Like, nobody got married in 1972. Nobody needed to and we didn't either. But we didn't need not to, you know. So, why not?"

Roger Patterson wasn't old-fashioned; like most fathers, he worried about his daughter. Preliminary screen test results were not good. No equalizer in the world could improve a voice that didn't have resonance to begin with, and as far as hitting the marks went, I was a fish out of water. The agency could have cut me loose and cut their losses, and Jill could have been shipped overseas, but once our affair leaked to the bowl people, they made an incredible offer. Triple, not double, for the two of us. We didn't even have to get married at halftime, just go through the parade-and-wave show. One of the hustlers persuaded the others that an ex-Rose Queen would turn their match-up of mediocre football teams into another Rose Bowl, so it made no sense not to give my charisma a trial.

Jill told all of this to Pearl and the reverend over ice cream, not even leaving out the part about her parents filing for divorce as soon as we were married.

"Nobody cares about image like Daddy. It's like they stayed together just so he could give me away, so things wouldn't look strange."

Pearl and the reverend didn't nod.

"We didn't have to lift a finger," she went on. "The agency rented a non-denominational chapel out on Long Island. Nobody came other than family and a few close friends. Kenny's parents came by boat from Connecticut, which was really elegant, but we didn't want to go overboard. It was all low-key, relaxed, informal. We didn't want the Olympic team."

"I had no close friends in sports, so that wasn't a problem," I said. "The food wasn't too cute and the Champagne wasn't from upstate New York. The ceremony didn't last too long and nobody got sick."

"I was Episcopalian, Kenny was Presbyterian, and the minister was a judge, so religion wasn't a problem."

"It was no problem at all," I said. "I couldn't have asked for a better wedding, even if it was my own."

We laughed and they were smiling and I didn't know how much I had drunk or how long we'd been talking about ourselves, only that dinner was over and it was time to go home. We hadn't found out much about them, but we had made it through. We enjoyed ourselves, and it wouldn't be far from the truth now when I said, "The reverend, I like him: he's good people!"

Although we never got around to having them over because they were too busy to come, we counted on Pearl and the reverend as friends. It wasn't until a few years later that I saw how boring we had been, how much they should have wanted to have nothing to do with us.

It wasn't still dark, but was more dark than light. We weren't hungover, even though the vodka from the night before was less than half full. Pounds of blankets kept us cozy as we argued whether it wouldn't be better to piss in bed than to get up and start a fire.

Miriam wanted breakfast, not olives and crabmeat, but the kind they used to have at the Busy Bee. The Busy Bee caught more damage than the stores, and I wondered if the cuteness of every part of the interior matching those striped curtains made it hard not to wreck. You didn't have to be a metallurgy engineer to wonder how it was possible to destroy a cast iron stove.

"Don't expect bacon and eggs," I said.

"Why not go back to the houses? One of them ought to have a kitchen that isn't ruined. We don't need power, with fireplaces and wood stoves."

"Breakfast could take all day," I said, but it wouldn't be hard to discourage her. We only had to go through the motions of survival for Miriam to get the idea that we could no longer stay.

There hadn't been a nuclear war and we weren't pioneers. She wouldn't talk money, but we had more than enough for a lavish splurge of motel living. Maybe this was her idea of a dry run for when we had nothing, as if you had to learn how to be destitute. Neither of us knew how to do anything. Even undemanding chores were too much for us. She could say we'd make do, but she had abandoned a building because she hadn't done any maintenance. Usually, things were the other way around, as the pride of ownership kept a place up while tenants didn't flinch to save it from falling down, but a lot of what we did was the other way around.

Anyone else might have made camp in this office over the saloon after first finding a way to keep the place warm, stove or no stove. From thick carpet to wood paneling, swivel chair to foldout couch, the office liquor cabinet revealed all in a reflection and nothing past the glass, except for a humidor full of cigars. Miriam couldn't resist lighting up as we sat down to jimmy the drawers.

"The way through a man's drawers is to his checkbook," she said, whipping it out to find the register filled with none but the names of women. They couldn't all have been waitresses. Even waitresses aren't waitresses, except in bad recurring dreams.

Another drawer had the usual stuff left over from lodge meetings, pipe smoking, World War II, and trips to places far away that a man hangs onto without thinking and can't notice years afterwards without thinking a lot more. I didn't want to disturb the stuff, but we needed matches. Among the pins and decals from the university were ticket stubs and an old football game program that might have been worth something in a baseball card shop if it had been from a year when the Sooners finished on top, and when I said I'd have to look it up, Miriam said she failed to see how anyone who knew the World Series winners and losers from every year since 1945 could not know the number one college football team in 1971.

"It's not the same," I said, adding that I didn't remember all the gold medallists from my own Olympic team. "You must have something you don't remember that others think you should never forget."

She was about to say, then didn't, so I told her that nobody was expected to remember them all, and in my case there hadn't been that many. They say your first should be unforgettable, if only because it's awful, but for me it wasn't because it wasn't and she was. Not that I was any better.

"Bet you can't remember all the presidents in your lifetime," I said.

"I even remember the vice-president runners who

didn't win: Kefauver, Lodge, Miller, Muskie, Shriver and Eagleton, Dole, Mondale, and Ferraro."

"Don't you forget anything you're supposed to know?"

"I don't even forget stuff I'm not supposed to know."

"That's not — "

"O.K., there's stuff I don't remember, like for instance, cigars make me sick."

At least the toilet wasn't out of order. This must have been a mistake. Even I knew what the cold could do to uninsulated pipes. Some years ago in Seattle, we learned that the hard way, which I mentioned to change the subject, but she couldn't think about Seattle without talking about Boyd, which meant talking about sex. She did her impression of Boyd shooting his wad, like I'd never heard it before.

"Ooooh, Jeeeeezusss, aurghnk nk nk," she said, "even a foxhole atheist like Boyd had to scream it. Tell you what, Chick, you are different: you don't yell Jesus when you come."

There was no stopping her. As Miriam went through the come shot calls of more guys than losing vice presidents, I couldn't help thinking how she'd remember me. Still, I had to act like it was no big deal. It wasn't always a breeze getting along with her, but I didn't want to rush the day when it would be impossible.

For now, it became impossible not to eat breakfast. Almost every house had a stash of oatmeal, powdered milk, and brown sugar, so we were no worse off than we'd have been in a fallout shelter. Boiling water on a wood stove took no time, and before we knew it, we were fed.

That wasn't all. More booze turned up where it didn't belong. Loose floorboards, fake walls, hollow stairs, and whole bookcases full of books that weren't books but bottles made you think you'd seen everything, until you saw something else.

"I don't know how they left this behind," she said.

"Maybe they didn't."

Sometimes it seemed that the agency didn't exist, that Roger Patterson used it only as a front, as if there were something else he really did, instead. Wasn't that how advertising was? He might have been some kind of vice-president, but he wasn't a major stockholder. I never met the top brass. They could have died and turned into trust funds managed by banks to support heirs who were no more deserving than we were.

I told Roger Patterson the reverend's idea about exposing Gold Medal Health Spas, but he didn't think it was funny. Not that he feared Jimmy Ray. He didn't want anyone to pull a *60 Minutes* on him. This was right after Watergate, when the press wasn't gutless.

"You know we haven't done anything wrong, and I know we haven't done anything wrong, but give them the hand-held shot jostled down a corridor and we've had it."

He didn't believe in justice.

"Innocent until proven guilty is the opposite of how it is, and you can say I'm terrible and call me a radical, but you know as well as I do that they don't even prosecute you if they can't win. And as far as I'm concerned, if they don't win, they do, because if it looks bad, it is bad. It's sad, when you consider, truly a tragedy, yet things do sort themselves out, and not only because we have seven million dollars."

"Come on, Daddy, we don't have seven million dollars. If we did, we wouldn't live in this shithole."

"Jill sweetheart, what have I told you about language: language is the, come on, don't be shy."

Together they said, "Language is the audio of image," but Jill didn't say it the same way he did.

"Don't you see the problem here? Jill honey, you have an objection, a complaint, a beef that may or may not be valid, and here we are sidetracked into recriminations that have nothing to do with the legitimacy of your objection, or, do they?"

"Image is the picture of reality," said Jill, not looking at anyone.

"The aphorism is the last refuge of a chauvinist," said Belinda, "but don't explain it or you kill the joke. And speaking of language, Rog, better can the beef or you'll come off like Joe Pyne, or wasn't it your fantasy to host a screaming maniac talk show?"

"Now that man," said Roger Patterson, "projects image purely for the sake of negative afterimage, which proves my point."

He never failed to prove his point, the point being a signal that argument had stopped (as if it had ever started), and so Belinda served.

We played doubles on the alternate hit rule, and while it was more ping pong than table tennis, none of us got as much exercise as we did during these games in our basement. One rule of the health club was that you couldn't play games. Never mind that ping pong was better for you than the Tone-o-matic, the idea was there could be no fun.

Since we were in charge, the rules didn't apply to us.

What Jill said about the seven million wasn't supposed to be mentioned, but it came up a lot. With the ball in play, though, only Belinda could talk (the rest of us had to concentrate so we wouldn't forget whose turn it was to hit). She didn't play better than we did. She didn't care if she made Roger lose.

"I don't know if this is the right time, but we got a call from Salinas about the machines. I wouldn't have thought much, except El Paso called the next day and it sounded like the same problem. These people are unbelievable. You tell them it's supposed to hurt, they complain when it doesn't hurt, and then when it does, they really complain. You can't say, 'relax baby, you're tense,' so I told them to tell the stiffs to eat less protein and if that doesn't work, to fast. Anyway, it's no biggie, but if it is, we might as well fold our tent and hit the road."

Roger Patterson didn't like us to call the clients "stiffs." Even in the basement under the thwocking of ping pong, the word stuck so that it might pop out when it shouldn't. Belinda said they wouldn't mind, that this was no different from the abuse kids get from gym teachers, but Roger Patterson believed all abuse should come from the program and that the instructors (the human element) should offer encouragement.

"Belinda, Belinda pet, Belinda, listen to me: you're not getting it. What we, what Gold Medal Health Spas is all about, in a nutshell, is life, not death. We do not say 'stiffs,' we say 'clients.' We treat our clients not as the 97-pound weaklings they were, but as the beautiful people they can be. And above all, we are not gym teachers. If nothing else, we are here to help our clients release themselves from the gym teacher-induced inhibitions and retrograde disciplinary mechanisms that thwart self-actualization."

"Don't talk, serve," said Jill.

"Don't talk, she says, but there is a perception, and Ken, Ken my man will back me up on this one, there is a perception that the only time I have your undivided attention is when I hold the ball."

"No shit, Roger, 8-14, serve already."

"It doesn't stop there," Belinda continued with the

game, "because after El Paso, we got a call from Key West. Roger, don't. It's not your turn."

"8-15," I said, "Roger didn't follow."

"Key West, she said, didn't you hear? Jill, I appeal to you, darling, did you not hear Key West? Belinda is absolutely correct, this is not a coincidence. I will go to Key West at once and then, one day, we'll look back on this and see that it wasn't so bad after all."

"We don't have a club in Key West, babe, I just thought you weren't paying attention," said Belinda.

"Belinda sweets, I can't get over my shame for a) going out of turn, and b) not developing the state of Florida to its full potential. Before I serve, let me say that the deprived are crying out for fitness and we cannot deny them. Florida should be our stronghold, what with Ken here no less than a Favorite Son, but aside from Tampa, where are we? And so Belinda, Jill doll, King Ken, don't let me off the hook, send me to Key West, force me to follow through on what I should have done long ago."

"In eighteen months," said Belinda, "we have grown so fast that we don't know what we make. We have 28 branches in 25 states, although only one in all of Florida because we can't afford the overhead in anyplace that isn't a swamp. Of course, if we had picked Fosterville and Key West like I said instead of that piece of Tampa that should have been redlined, we might not need to feed off the franchise fees. Not that I don't support deprivation, but we go out of the way to pick out-of-the-way places. Don't tell me about cheap rent. We could be losing money and never learn, as long as we keep opening branches and charging fees. So Rog, by all means go to Key West, and while you're at it, hit Gretna, Lynchburg, Altoona, and everywhere in between, since the base of this pyramid can't be too broad."

Roger Patterson played up close and tried to smash, I stayed back to catch his put-aways with a slice, Belinda lunged forward to pick up the backspin, and Jill kept the rally alive, as if to set up her father for his best shot to show him it wasn't good enough.

"Hold it, time out, whoa," he put down his paddle, "my partner has raised a question that can't go unanswered. Isn't there a smack of hostility to all this?"

"Not again," said Jill.

"There: mumbling, backbiting, the treachery of unrest. Negative thinking. Gold Medal Health Spas is not about negative thinking. Hostility is not progress but regression, the enemy of growth. We are, therefore we grow, for to not grow is to be — "

"There's no business like grow business."

"Don't interrupt. We are not crooks. And, I know you don't mean that, but image, kids, image. People hear 'pyramid' and they think Egypt, camels, tombs — no, they think scams, chain letters, fraud. Thousands, no, millions have been invested here, not by Ma and Pa out of their savings but by the agency. The risk is ours and the loss won't be theirs. And Jill, Belinda, Ken, neither will the GAIN."

He wouldn't quit until we agreed with him.

In late afternoon the sound of engines sent Miriam and me behind an undefaced wall. We wanted to be near the car, even if we couldn't hope to outrun them.

They weren't what we expected. The motorcycles weren't larger than scooters. We should have figured they'd ride bikes that went off-road, but we didn't figure they would be sensible enough to wear helmets. Not only that, they had sleeping bags and backpacks, camping stoves and tents. You couldn't exactly picture them pissing their names on doors.

"Oh no," said Miriam. "I wouldn't be surprised if there's a photographer to put them in some catalog. Nothing that's not right off the rack."

"Don't look now: they all have cameras."

"It can't be a shoot."

"Nah, it's probably just the weekend. Don't worry, they'll be gone by early Sunday. They don't look like a group to skip church."

They couldn't have been the crew that rewired the Tone-o-matic, destroyed the Busy Bee, and set the beer can fires. They didn't pay much attention to the town, except to use it as a backdrop for snaps of each other. Maybe they were models on holiday, running around in comp camping outfits, glad not to be under some director's control, but I remembered what Belinda had said about what she and her model pals did for fun. Whatever they were, I didn't want to make the mistake many do when sizing up others who show some similarity to themselves, to think that they were just like me. Not the way I was now but the way I had been then. As usual, I got the feeling that one might have recognized me, especially if any of them had a link to the agency, but from where we sat, they had the generic good looks that made them indistinguishable from dozens of faces I had worked with. They were obviously harmless, but I didn't want to move, even if it couldn't matter if they did recognize me. And yet, I couldn't stop thinking how someone who knew me then would react to me these days.

They were doing things they shouldn't have wanted anyone to see. I felt sorry for them and didn't want to give away our position. How long would it take for them to get it out of their systems, for the piercing echoes of those squeals to disappear and the image of those charades to shut up? Miriam might have counted her bless-

ings that she had never been like that, but she only
shook her head in disbelief.

"They can't think they're clever," she said. "Nobody
is that clever."

"They're insecure. Nothing can't be ironic because
sincerity is vulnerable. Isn't there a little of that in all of
us?"

"A little's not the same as a lot."

I couldn't deny it. I wasn't just a latent model. I had
frolicked through my share of promos, real and unreal.
Although we weren't looking at me out there, dancing,
sticking out my tongue, bending over, and generally acting like a fucking idiot in a rock band on TV, I had to
apologize.

"Aw Chick, you couldn't help it."

"I didn't just keep to myself and a bunch a friends,
I was on the air."

The six of them had stripped to bicycle tights, even
though the temperature wasn't much over freezing. The
men giggled like girls, but they weren't patsies. Exercise
machines nowadays weren't what they used to be, back
when manual labor built bodies as well as any training
program could. You might wrestle transmissions for
minimum wage and still not get the muscles these folks
had from gym work.

"I mean, I was part of the culture, no different from
the Pocket Fisherman."

After a few more poses, they hit the saloon without
bothering to check out the other buildings. I didn't care
whether their cooler was full of beer or soda pop or
what brand of gum they chewed, we could hang out on
the other side of town and nobody would know. If only
Miriam hadn't run out of cigarettes.

"Bet you anything they don't smoke."

"Oh no? They're right off the back of a glossy magazine, making that menthol scene as if they weren't a bunch of oatmeal brains."

"You're not serious — better to shit upstream against the wind with your head stuck under water."

"Human nature, Chick, they won't refuse us. They'll bend over backwards to keep it nice, no matter what we do. They'll be begging to give us cigarettes, beer, anything to keep us happy, and we leave without paying."

I didn't like it. If she wanted to socialize, though, why not let her? Playing out the possibilities of action couldn't fail to get us back on the road, the sooner the better. This encounter might show her what we were missing, even if what we were missing amounted to no more than shaking down strangers in bars.

Miriam wanted to wait for them to settle in, so we could make an entrance, but we couldn't arrive late or they would have more of a claim to the joint than we did. The idea was to uncover that we had been here, heard them, and eventually bothered to see what they wanted. Not that there was any point in fine-tuning our entrance.

Miriam had kept her black wedding dress from getting dirty, and when I looked at her it was hard not to see how you take someone close to you for granted. She wasn't only beautiful, she had an attitude that took charge, making you think that by being with her, you were more important than you were.

We waited for sunset, which didn't take long. It was overcast, with a pearly glow that told us the blizzard wouldn't wait. The wind had picked up, so we didn't hear the music until we reached the door.

"We can't go through with this," I said.

"Why not?"

"'I Can't Help But Wonder Where I'm Bound': folk songs."

All irony stopped when they started to sing, and no matter how they strained to mimic the original, you could tell this was no parody. The voices were clenched in harmony, with an edge of conviction that gave you the feeling this was no place to be bumming cigarettes. Even though they didn't sound bad, there was a sense that they thought they sounded great, if only because the song carried a special meaning for them. I couldn't knock it. So it hadn't worked for me, so what. But Miriam wasn't just after smokes.

They didn't stop all at once. We walked in no differently than we would have into any bar. A nod took care of greetings, and they didn't stare at us as much as glance at each other until, one by one, voices broke.

"—where I'm bound, where I'm bound, and I can't—"

Throats cleared as they do when nobody wants to speak.

"Aw, don't stop on our account," said Miriam.

"We didn't think anyone was here," said the guy with the guitar.

Some giggled; some didn't. Nobody's eyes went the same way, giving us room to examine them. They were older and younger than we were, and since jewelry wasn't their style, those had to be wedding rings on their fingers. Back home, at some town that hadn't died, their kids were probably staying with other families. This was a retreat, a chance for them to get together with old friends and do things they used to do when they were young and liked to pretend they were free spirits, so they didn't need a couple of creeps gaping at them like everything they stood for was stupid.

"Different songs for different gongs, ain't that right? Come on, you play and I'll sing," said Miriam, "and if you come up with one I don't know, I'll buy you a drink."

"You better not lose," I said.

"No problem, I know more folk songs than losing vice-president come shots. I used to date one: not the song but the singer."

"What if they don't pick a folk song?"

The chords sounded Irish if not Scottish and the hook was pure Hollywood. Sentimental and upbeat, moving in a mournfully peppy sort of way, it was the amalgam we should have guessed he would not only perform, but write. He stared at Miriam and his friends couldn't keep from snickering.

"Give up?" he said, but he couldn't sing before Miriam belted it out with a brogue so phony it would curdle scones.

Note for note she matched him, no matter how he faltered, with the most immaculately obscene lyrics you could imagine. I couldn't get over it. She didn't miss a rhyme, and everything made sense. Anyone who had ever tried to fake lyrics might say there was no cheaper fill than sex for the blanks, but Miriam's rap was so complete and complex that you would swear she hadn't just ad-libbed her way through a tune this guy thought of as his alone. It wasn't the filthiest song I ever heard and it even had a happy ending, but it wasn't their idea of a good time.

"Oh no," said the woman next to the guitar player, touching his arm, "that's not — "

The others tried to shut her up; she wouldn't.

"Billy Boy," she said, repeating it until we got the idea she meant not the singer but the song. "That's not 'Billy Boy.'"

Belinda didn't exaggerate when she said we grew too fast. A month couldn't go by without us taking off for some corner of the country in order to open a branch spa. We were supposed to be a group of beautiful people who would make everyone envious, even though these towns had no use for us.

I never got used to how polite the locals were. Sure, we promised a few jobs and plenty of flesh, and we were polite to them, but couldn't they see through us? Our bodies wouldn't last fifteen minutes in a grain mill or a corn field. Whatever goodwill my gold medals bought couldn't help being swapped for scorn once they saw how flimsy our operation was. Pretending to be more than what you were wasn't something people should put up with, and we came on like a carnival crossed with a USO show. Maybe they didn't hold it against us because they saw how they weren't the ones to be swindled, so the enterprise had less to do with making us rich than with keeping them entertained.

The first reports of back injuries should have slowed our growth, but none of us wanted to admit the spas were doomed. Nothing beat the opening of a new branch for making you feel wanted, even as you suspected that nobody ever liked disco music, that people only subjected themselves to it so they could get laid.

Thanks to Roger Patterson, we let a modest presentation turn into a tasteless spectacle. It was his idea to jazz things up, which had nothing to do with jazz. In the first shows, Jill and I merely appeared in sweatsuits, took our bows, and shook a few hands while an emcee who knew how not to bore a crowd kept things moving. To Roger Patterson, this wasn't enough. Not enough audio, not enough image, not enough Roger Patterson. A fifteen-minute ribbon cutting blew into an endless extravaganza. Roger Patterson was no Mick Jagger, but he tried to be. He even stole a Rolling Stones song for his theme, retooling the tempo with a rhythm machine and changing the title to his favorite line to yell at women busting their asses while he gripped their thighs, "No mercy."

At least Jill and I didn't have much to do, although there was a threat to have me take on any rube who wanted to race my backstroke with his crawl. While Roger Patterson bounced around and lipsynched, we stood and smiled until, little by little, we took off our sweats and stretched, a coy maneuver that functioned as a kind of carelessly informal strip tease.

I should have welcomed the opportunity to go all over the country and meet a variety of people and places, but a small town in New Mexico seemed no different from a small town in Tennessee, once you got past the plants. As a franchise, Gold Medal Health Spas wasn't in business to promote local color. We might recognize where we were with an icon here or there — a cactus in Yuma, a lobster in Orono — because it sent the message that you couldn't keep going back to the same branch if you wanted to train in the full range of atmospheres and altitudes. Customers were reassured, though, that no matter where they went, they would find a reliable level of service and amenities. Aside from symbols and scenery, you didn't get a lot of local color in an environment rigged for deprivation.

We should have appreciated how Roger Patterson treated each demo as an independent creative act, but it was nerve wracking not to know what he would do next. There was no script. If there was, only he knew it, like a touch football play where the quarterback says no more than, "Go out." Jill and I were there to be manipulated, and the Flexettes couldn't help exercising in unison, since they had done the act thousands of times.

A tape full of songs covered by a combo that played Holiday Inns along the beltways of unimportant cities gave Roger Patterson his inspiration. He wouldn't let

anyone mess with the tape and he alone pushed PLAY
and PAUSE. Like many who take over center stage,
Roger didn't have a great voice and he wasn't especially tall or strong or handsome. He wasn't even that
clever. We often thought of good lines that he missed the
second before he said something dull, but we couldn't
criticize, because he was on center stage and we
weren't. He was simply because he was, we weren't
because he was, and we weren't because we weren't.
That's how Belinda put it when she said why she never
went along.

"He's better off without me."

"But I'll have no one to talk to," said Jill, indirectly
referring to me.

"Some day, babe, you're going to ask yourself
whether it isn't worth staying home, but it's going to
take another ten years before you do it. Or, you could do
it now without thinking, and regret it the rest of your
life."

Belinda didn't say what to do as much as suggest
what to avoid. Jill went along as if she had no choice, and
before we knew it, we were on stage again in the parking lot of another supermarket on the outskirts of a town
I don't remember in a year I get confused because it was-
n't an Olympiad. It had to be after the "Do the thing that
makes her sing" commercial because Roger Patterson
wasted no time getting the Flexettes to chant this as they
did leg-lifts. Patriotism wasn't yet back in, but it wasn't
the kill-sell it had been a few years earlier, so Roger
Patterson worked to a medley of discotized Cohan. At
first it was amazing how the synthesizer could make any
song go into any other song, but after a while you got so
used to it that when a real band pulled it off, you took it
for a shameless stunt. Anyway, while the Flexettes
chanted the latest slogan between pants, Roger Patterson

whipped "Yankee Doodle Dandy" into "Grand Old Flag" until "Danke Schoen," the *Wide World of Sports* theme, the Olympic fanfare, and "Du Weiss Nicht Gut Ich Dir Bin" made it obvious where we were headed.

Roger Patterson couldn't count on us to follow him, so our cues were our names. It surprised me that he waited so long to call us and it must have pissed off the Flexettes, even if they did no more than jog in place. When he did, he called Jill and not me. She had to lock in a smile so nobody would see how she hated to "do the meat routine" alone. She snapped off her sweats like a pro, though, and when she bent over stretching to face the audience, you wouldn't know that she faced the wrong way.

Roger didn't stop. The benefits of training and self-discipline led to pride and satisfaction until, out of nowhere, the tape played the call from another announcer, the call of my last race. Roger Patterson didn't need to say my name: the old broadcast had it loud and clear.

When I stripped, the crowd went nuts — not a few guys would have loved to draw such a reaction by standing on stage in a star-spangled tank suit. The Flexettes closed in and fanned out again, circling arms backward one after another in a move you wouldn't see unless you saw it from above. Someone uncovered a pedestal, and although I was flattered, climbing it gave me the creeps.

Twisted by the disco beat, the next song didn't sound like one that people would stand up and take off their hats for. Roger Patterson handed Jill a box, and without hesitating, she reached to drape the ribbon around me. I had to bend — even those sprinters in Mexico City had to bend — but when I stood again, there was no way I could raise a fist in protest or do anything but what the unscripted directions said.

Unlike the anthems in recent Olympics, which had
been put into short forms so the ceremonies didn't out-
last the events, the disco anthem went on and on. First
Roger Patterson, then the Flexettes, and finally everyone
in the Food Boy parking lot chanted:

> "Land of the free, home of the brave
> No mercy, no mercy
> Land of the free, home of the brave
> No mercy, no mercy."

We left with our hands clamped to each others'
hands while they cheered, and I was grateful to Roger
Patterson for not making me play it straight.

"Wasn't it worth the look on his face?" said Miriam.

Sarcastically, I said it was, but I wasn't angry, even
though we couldn't ask the only people we had seen for
days to help us when our car wouldn't start. Any
moment a snowstorm would make it impossible to
leave, and there wasn't enough food and booze to keep
us here. There was almost no more firewood. If we
managed to get the car started, we didn't know where
to go. The tires were bald and we had no chains. The
radio was busted and I didn't like how my clothes
smelled. The pipes didn't drain any more and the toilets
were full. Life was bad but not dull because suddenly
there was a good chance we would die. Thirst, starva-
tion, exposure, disease; boredom, hate, fear: I didn't
worry. I had Miriam and Miriam had money and at last
she didn't want to be here.

We went from junker to junker, popping hoods for
batteries and using pliers for a wrench before it was too
dark to tell the minus from the plus. With the first flurries, we found a live one, and then we didn't have to
wait.

We drove to the house where Miriam got the dress, so she could exchange it for sweaters, past the folksinging models, who hadn't left the bar. As for the rewired Tone-o-matic altar, we figured it was one of those mysteries that are best left unsolved. With ghost towns, how many official explanations don't conceal what really went wrong?

Our stopover in Booth wasn't much different from the rest of our recent decisions. We did what we thought would be fun, only to discover we had wasted our time accomplishing nothing. If we learned a lesson, fine, but one dead end didn't look like another until you had to turn around.

We didn't need a map or a route sign. The wind out of the northwest pointed our way along the only road leaving town, and as the flurries thickened into solid clouds, it felt good not to be stuck where we had been.

"Don't you love a fresh start, Chick?"

"Too bad we don't have more gas."

We hadn't siphoned what we could from the junkers, leaving us to hope for a town with an all-night truck stop. And how many gas stations still carried gas that wasn't unleaded?

"Once I read about a boat on Lake Erie that ran out of gas in a storm," she said, "but that didn't stop them. They fed two gallons of booze to the engine, and damned if that sucker didn't burn like a champ."

Weeds rolled like waves in the headlights through the whiteness of the dark, and although the wind wasn't against us, gusts rocked worse than bumps from below. The wheel had limitless play, making it like a ship's wheel in cartoons where, to make the slightest turn, they sent it spinning. Yet for all the bouncing, we never bottomed out. The road was our channel without measurable depth.

In order to steer, we didn't see road as much as what wasn't road, the wavy weeds. Slickness wasn't a problem, without bends or hills. Neither of us knew enough about driving through blizzards to say how much was too much. I didn't slow down, but floored it, to put as much as possible between here and there.

"Bet that you can't guess what I want for Christmas, Chick."

"Christmas could come without us knowing."

"Chick, be nice, we weren't there more than three days. If it had been a nuclear war, you wouldn't bitch about any three days."

"At least the radiation rots your memory and you don't think so much as hallucinate. That's not what you want for Christmas, is it?"

"I'm not telling, now."

"You don't have to. It can't be anything but a pony."

"You piece of shit," she unveiled a grin. "I didn't talk in my sleep, did I?"

"Come on, you don't really want a pony."

"Don't I?"

"Where are you gonna keep a pony and what are you going to do with him: not ride him, I hope."

"Not a pony, jackass, a horse: a racehorse."

This wasn't the first we had said of it, so I should-n't have been surprised. After all, Hawaii had been a fly-by-night whim compared to the day in, day out revolving beacon of an urge she had to get into the racing game, an urge that never went away, a lure that was also a warning. We took turns bringing up the subject, in a guilty pleasure tone that made the likelihood of her actually going through with it comfortably out of reach, so I attached no meaning to whatever she said about it.

Now, unfortunately, she could afford one. Not just the claiming tag, but the trainer, stable rent, and feed and vet bills she had taken off the tables in Reno. For a while, we could be big shots at some podunk track, turf-clubbing it up until they threw us out and told us never to return. Probably the urge would go away again, yet it bothered me how I wasn't as hot on the idea as she was.

I was more bothered, though, by the thought of Texas, where a lot of suits had been filed that named none other than me as the main defendant. One speeding ticket there, and it would be far worse than, do not pass go, do not collect $200. But then, all over the country, backs could be blowing out like time bombs, forcing absentee judgments where all I never made would be given away to the injured, thanks to the expert testimony of chiropractors.

I couldn't say that bankruptcy made me a bum. After the lawyers rigged it so we could walk, I still did my agency gig, and after Jill left and they fired me, I had to do something so I wouldn't go hungry. Some deadbeats went from bankruptcy to bankruptcy, skimming personal fortunes while sending investors and customers to hell, but it wasn't in me to operate that way. I hadn't the morals or the skill of someone like the reverend. To me, bankruptcy only made it pointless to earn more than it took to get by.

Although we say "get by" like we could live on diddly, you wouldn't believe how much it cost to keep out of the gutter.

Or how much luck it took to keep out of the gutter, if you were driven by a blizzard along a highway without markers. After an hour, we went no faster than 35. Nothing was open. Going through towns deader than Booth, we saw no reason to stop. We couldn't ignore the map any longer, because we doubted the two things we had agreed on: that it wasn't yet Arkansas or Thanksgiving.

Launched by the unexpected success of that Florida bowl game, my career and the health club chain took off in spite of my doubts. Rather than wonder about it, I figured it was a case of the abnormal being normal. I trusted people not to dump on me, at least at the beginning, and they never did. Since I got more breaks than the average person, I knew the good times would have to end sometime, but this sense of awareness didn't degenerate into outright dread. Maybe that's because it was so great not having to make decisions. Go with the flow didn't sound half bad to a guy who had spent thousands of hours forcing his way through water.

I might have thought Roger Patterson was a jerk, that his schemes were ridiculous and that it was a mistake to let him use me, but guys like Roger Patterson ruled the world. Maybe he was a little more crass than most operators, but anybody would recognize the logos, slogans, and jingles he had used to create a want for things unneeded. Some of the other campaigns he had masterminded lived on for decades, making their businesses seem not like passing fads but cultural touchstones. He wasn't insincere in his devotion to Gold Medal Health Spas. Even as the franchise went downhill, he didn't cut and run. He offered to buy more shares of the company, which was taken for a show of confidence, so nobody sold. In the end, he insisted the spas had hurt him more than they had hurt anyone who wound up in traction, fooling nobody.

Gold Medal was neither his first flop nor his biggest. The cutthroat nature of the advertising racket made the agency kingpins brag more about the winery fiasco, the airline crash, and the folly of Shangri-La than they did about empires he had created against all odds, as if anyone could have seen the potential in travelers checks, running shoes, or a battlefield theme park called

No Man's Land. The undoing of his career had more to do with timing than with the failure of the spas. The agency had made it clear that, after a series of disappointments, he was too old to be given another chance, but that this would be an exception. If not for the marriage of Jill to me and my medals, would they have sent him packing?

I couldn't see how anyone could stand a guy who talked through his nose, and in the beginning it was my feeble imitation of her father that drew Jill to me, that coaxed her to unload how she felt about the agency. Of course, resisting him by pretending to hope for the collapse of the spas wasn't a very sound basis for a marriage. But we didn't care. Money was meaningless, we were irresponsible, and nothing made sense. As we headed for Booth, we celebrated with the giddy self-confidence that came from a success we reckoned to be unmatchable, so that everything that happened next would occur happily ever after.

Behind us, huge white vans sparkling with chrome rolled into town, and when they unfurled the cameras, lights, and crates, it appeared the locals were in for a few days of having their lives disrupted by shooting schedules and the cheap thrill of being able to tell what somebody famous really seems to be. With Roger Patterson not due to arrive until later, Belinda persuaded the agency to hire roustabouts to handle the move. We didn't have to do anything, not even supervise, as all of that got done by union crews that normally put up sets for situation comedies.

The headquarters had been built but was left unfinished. The windows couldn't open except by a special wrench. By mistake, they filled the pool with chlorine before connecting the vents, so nobody could go inside without a gas mask. This was June, a hundred in the sun, and the locals said, "You ain't seen nothing yet."

Hot summers, cold winters, droughts with mosqui-
toes, storms without rain, hail you never felt before, and
tornados across the endless rolling plains made this a
Biblical wilderness or a planet without ozone.
Unaccustomed as we were to this place, we somehow
earned the respect of the locals by choosing this for a
place to live. Mostly, they were older, and the few that
still had kids in school sent them fifty miles by bus to
get there, while the others didn't hope that their grown
sons and daughters would return, except to bury them.
They stared, but who wouldn't stare? And they didn't
say a word when we tried to explain our business.

"It's sort of like a McDonalds or Holiday Inn," I said,
"but more like those resorts where people take vacations
so they won't go to seed. You work hard, and at the end
of the day, you rest, but these folks aren't like you. They
have desk jobs, they may do no more than walk from the
parking lot to the office. They get out of shape and they
don't like it. They want to look good and feel good, and
by the time they realize how far they've let themselves
go, they can't even play softball. These are people who
don't think they're doing enough unless they make a big
sacrifice. It's not enough for them to get up at five AM
to jog. Well, five might not seem very early to you, but if
you don't have to be to work until eight or nine, the
alarm rings at five and it's the middle of the night."

"It's not just look good, all right?" said Jill. "It's that,
you know, you see those movie magazines, actresses on
TV, posters on billboards, and you want to, um, not
look like that maybe, but look more like that than the
way you do look. Not that you don't look fabulous. I
mean, you look about as good as a person should want
to look, but these are people who'll pay to look better
than they would if they didn't go ahead and throw

themselves into something like this. Think of plastic surgery without the knife."

Nobody seemed to mind. All around us sat survivors of run-ins with farm machines, whose plastic surgeries hadn't been fanny tucks.

"What you see when you watch the tube, go to the movies, or when the commercials come on," said Belinda, "is nothing but a show. There's a story maybe or a scene of what you'd like to do, where you'd like to be, with somebody you wouldn't mind, ah, being with. Say it's a scene in, I don't know, Hawaii. On one level, it's pretty, with palm trees, hammocks, beach, water, flowers, drinks out of pineapples, the works, but it doesn't stop there. You want to be there, to make the scene, to get into it, and you can't come as you are. You have to change, to go through some process to undo whatever may be holding you back from getting from here to there."

"I haven't been to Hawaii since the war," said one, and the others nodded.

As we went back to the house after the set designer and movers had gone, Belinda assured us, "They couldn't not understand. They just haven't dealt with our kind of flex."

We walked around the house pulling out drawers and opening closets, but nothing was out of place. Meanwhile, the picture window in the living room buckled, no matter how light the wind. We couldn't remember the tornado window rule (open or shut?). None of us was remotely familiar with the Great Plains, and we hadn't thought much of what life would be like in a tiny Oklahoma town.

Midway through the ceremonial dinner of whiskey and T-bones, Belinda said she wasn't much of a beef cook. She wouldn't ruin a slab of meat, but she wanted us to understand she wasn't a range queen: "The Dale Evans bit I can do without."

Rather than try to learn about this place from westerns filmed in Spain, Belinda said she tried to read Wright Morris, but liked his novels set in Brooklyn and in Mexico better than the ones set in Nebraska, where "nothing happens." We hadn't come here for the cattle, the geology, the paleontology, or the wheat. We came here not for what it was but for what it was not. Not Hollywood, New York, New Orleans, Germany, or whatever.

The agency told us to be ourselves, which meant not to load up on cowboy hats on the coast in order to show the natives we belonged. The whole scene was so ludicrous, by the time Roger Patterson arrived, we couldn't have been sillier. We weren't high, but he must have felt that he'd come late to a party that took off without him. We couldn't say anything without giggling. Usually, he was the grinning optimist and we were nothing if not skeptical of his grandiose projections.

He didn't laugh with us. Knowing Belinda's history, he couldn't believe that she hadn't slipped, slipping us something to take us with her.

We didn't care what he believed.

"Roger, man," I said (I never called anyone "man"), "check out the weeds. You've never seen such weeds."

"No kidding, Daddy, they're everywhere. You don't notice, and there they are."

"Jill sweetie, Ken, settle down, folks, let's review some of the Dos and Don'ts."

"Come on, Rog, Dos and Don'ts?" said Belinda.

"You might think they're not flowers," I said, "but the way they turn colors, it's just wild."

"They're wild, they should be free," said Jill, stunning us by how funny this was, in a code nobody else could understand.

"Wild and free," said Belinda, and we couldn't stop laughing all over again.

"Number one," said Roger, "no drugs.

"Number two, there shall be no act without full regard for image. Don't breathe without thinking, how do I look, is someone watching, am I projecting the positivity consistent with the goals of the program?

"Number three, thou shalt not — "

"No prob, Rog," I put my arm around him and led him to the door. It was something I never did, but was always done to me. At the moment, it didn't seem out of line. He wasn't in control; I was.

We went out into what would have been the yard and kept going until we were in the middle of the unfathomable wildflowers.

"Dig it, man, can't you — "

"No. I'm sorry, but it's not working, Ken. I love you like a son and I appreciate that this, this gesture, is in some way a tribute to what you think should be said and done, an homage to image, but, and I say this out of respect and with all due affection, you are not that. And that's good, because I'm not saying you can't bring it off, but, trust me, the man-dig-it-flower-child thing is a no go. It won't sell, they won't buy. The counterculture has moved on and really, I can't tell you how important this is, how much it means to be able to tell you that Ken, you don't need it. The hippie thing isn't, wasn't, and won't be for you and for that we're ever grateful. Let me be the one to say that you are better than that, that you are why we are here because without you, Champ, there would be no Gold Medal Health Spas."

He had his arm around me and we faced not the weeds, but the house, town, and headquarters of the empire to come.

-2

We hadn't thought of Arkansas as a destination, but crossing a state line gave the new state a significance that otherwise didn't apply. Miriam noticed how the snow seemed to stop at the border, the blizzard turning northeastward as we went south through an ice storm that didn't make the road any safer. Whatever faulty connection there was inside the radio inexplicably fixed itself, so it came on and went off regardless of what we did to the dials. We were told not to travel unless it was necessary. Well, nothing was open but the road, and if we pulled over in order to wait out the storm, the heater would quit and we'd freeze to death.

I promised Miriam breakfast at one of those places that made your blood run pink because, after all, wasn't this the Razorback State? We got incredibly hungry at the thought of pigs. With every farmhouse along the road filling the dawn with smells of bacon, sausage, and ham, we didn't know how long we could hold out for the perfect cafe.

"Not that one: too new," said Miriam, at the first place that wasn't closed. She didn't have to explain. It was also too close to the interstate, so the cars in the lot were mostly from far away and packed full of families gone numb from hundreds of miles, who would never return to complain about a bad cup of coffee.

A good cup of coffee wasn't easy to define in a perfect cafe. You didn't expect good coffee, like the stuff off a decent espresso cart or the beans from a special coffee store. Any cafe that went that far in the coffee department couldn't be trusted to come across with the right level of lard off the griddle. Then again, you didn't want swill, the weak, the overheated, the burnt, or the java that tasted plain awful. So you might say that it was enough for coffee in a perfect cafe simply to be not bad. Not bad meant good.

Funny how coffee, the most important part of any cafe, didn't have to be great for people to say it was, since what they meant was, "Thanks for not making it terrible." Nothing served in these roadhouses had to be much more than tolerable. Not that flavor didn't matter, or that food wasn't as important as atmosphere. Things had to balance, or you'd have a rotten meal and feel that you had wasted time and money on stuff that was neither good nor good for you.

"Not that one: it stinks," said Miriam.

Not the cafe; the town. Downwind from a pulp mill, the cafe might have had everything else going for it, from the right cars to the dated design, but nobody with a nose should have chosen to eat here.

"All right, I didn't want to do this," I pulled over.

"Aw Chick, not here."

"Not here; here."

There on the map I pointed with a finger so round, she couldn't see where I meant.

"The place might not still be around, but the breakfasts were unbeatable."

"You knew a perfect cafe and you didn't beam in on it?"

"Not a cafe; a spa," I said. "Not necessarily a fat farm, at least not in the usual sense."

Hog Springs wasn't a famous Arkansas spa, but in 1973 the agency chose to study it as a model of everything Gold Medal had to avoid. Hog Springs didn't force customers to sacrifice, it indulged them. People ate all they wanted of the unhealthiest food, got up at their leisure and took plenty of naps. The gimmick was, no harm they did to themselves couldn't be treated by the water of the springs in the natural steam baths. The hot sulfur filtered through the pines was supposed to be an improved kind of air, so all you had to do was breathe to feel better, never minding how tainted it smelled. People staggered around hyperventilating, and went off like geysers, spewing hallelujahs without warning.

The pamphlets made a big deal about farm fresh eggs, cornfed pigs, and inorganic vegetables (sprayed so they wouldn't be contaminated by insects). Pictures showed customers doing nothing other than sleeping and eating, unless hanging out at the baths counted as doing something. Nobody came to Hog Springs to lose weight. They came to be told they didn't have to.

For some, Hog Springs was a healthy break in routine, in that no booze was allowed. And nobody would have dropped dead from too much exercise. A mud-immersion beauty treatment came at no extra charge, but then the total cost of getting fed and pampered for a week was ridiculously low.

Give the people all they want for as little as possible was the opposite of take all you can from them while giving little in return, but a spa was a spa, no matter how you operated. Decisions of what buildings went where and how many toilets to install were no different for a spa than for a summer camp, for that matter. How many people to hire, what supplies to buy, billing and reservation procedures, and the hundreds of other details you didn't think about until you were up against them kept the agency occupied for a long weekend.

Jill and I didn't have to be there, but not being there would have been uncooperative. For one thing, my appearance in Hog Springs soon after winning the gold in Munich paid our way, even if they weren't allowed to use pictures of me eating breakfast to promote their operation for longer than a month. The agency was afraid to endorse a competitor too close to the opening of our chain, as if potential customers couldn't handle the fact that America's twin symbols of fitness, Jill and I, might not be inclined to be more active than a couple of pandas.

More than fifteen years later, Miriam and I pulled into the driveway that toured the grounds on a whiff of the smokehouse, and when we reached the main entrance, it seemed nothing had changed. Business was busy as ever, even if this wasn't spa season. Spa season kicked in after the holidays and didn't quit until fall. Of course, breakfast was a year-round sport, but Hog Springs had to cling to the idea that gobbling 8000 fat-packed calories a day between sessions in the steam was the way to recover from the usual excesses of an unhealthy life.

This was the secret of the spa's success, even if nobody believed it. Thousands of restaurants flopped every day, and as good as the food was at Hog Springs, there were those who would say it wasn't good enough. When Jill and I were there, it shocked me that this place passing itself off as a spa got by with a state health rating of Grade D, yet customers had to believe that the low rating and greasy food meant less than the pictures of celebrities smiling from behind platters of ribs at the family style tables, no matter how many coronary by-pass operations would later catch up to those stars.

Wherever they came from, none of the cars in this lot looked as scummy as ours. Power windows, grooved tires, hubcaps, vanity plates, unchipped paint, and interiors you could have slept in like sleeping in a swank motel were typical. As for the owners, nobody was younger than sixty or less than sixty pounds overweight. Feeling out of place was no big deal, though. Nowhere did we not feel out of place, so to go somewhere and fit in would have been weird. Who cared, as long as we didn't pester anyone? We would pay our way and not talk too loud. We wouldn't ogle them or resent them for ogling us.

"No shoes, no shirt, no service," said the sign above the most recent Grade D certificate, and even though it wasn't summer, the desk clerk made a point of looking at our feet. Before he could say, "No vacancy," we said we only wanted breakfast.

There were no menus. A girl dressed in a sailor suit led the way into the dining room past rows of people eating so seriously, they wouldn't look up. She said we could have all we wanted and the food cart would arrive soon and regularly, but we shouldn't miss the cummer-bobble. We said we wouldn't, whatever it was.

Then there was something else not to miss.

"Don't say a word," I said.

"You think they won't notice?"

"Not if we don't."

Miriam wasn't convinced, and she was damned if she wouldn't check it out. She told the girl where we had to sit: at the end of the table that was under the picture of me from 1972, blown up unnaturally to actual size in a tank suit. I was glad she didn't laugh. Of all the spas in Arkansas, we had to pick the one that didn't just have portraits of country singers, movie cowboys, and favorite sons.

While she looked at me, I looked at the others, and there was Spike, with a bat on his shoulder and a smile uncomplicated by the bonehead play he made (or, would later make) that lost a pennant. Spike was so young, you couldn't picture him acting in a beer commercial filmed in a casino. None of these portraits were of anyone old. We were all on the way up, in our prime, and our names weren't listed, as if these mattered less than what we had done, which didn't compare to what we would become.

"I never noticed Spike, but he must have been here in 1973."

"Don't change the subject," said Miriam, and the way she stared left no doubt what the subject was.

"Jeez, too bad I wasn't a ballplayer. At least they don't have to hang out practically naked."

Under the table she felt up my thighs, making it hard not to feel full of myself.

"Whoa ho, at least one muscle hasn't turned to fat."

"They're not supposed to have it up. You don't suppose we should sue them for breakfast?"

Miriam wasn't listening while she kept looking from me to me.

Cummerbobbles were sausages, deep fat fried in batter, like corn dogs, except the batter wasn't cornmeal. The food tasted so good, you didn't notice how filling it was until you wanted to explode. Knowing in advance didn't stop you. Buttermilk pancakes, three kinds of ham, four kinds of sausage, scrambled eggs in bacon grease, bacon, grits, home fries, ham biscuits, sausage biscuits, biscuits in gravy, cinnamon rolls, and toast with strawberry jam made the oatmeal irrelevant, except nothing went so well with the local honey. Even coffee wouldn't save you.

The coffee was strong enough to cut through it all; in 1973, I couldn't take it without cream. Real cream: no substitutes. I used to make a game of trying to undo the years of training. No all-you-can-eat spread was big enough, no sausage was raunchy enough, and no matter what I ate, the coffee pulled the body through.

With the agency paying, I never held back. The greatest feature of my body wasn't that it could go backwards through water freakishly fast, but whatever I ate, it burned. With some effort, I could look like that poster boy, particularly since I didn't feel the same about food these days.

The breakfast was a nutritionist's nightmare, whether or not you ate five times as much as you should. I ate like a snake, like I didn't believe Miriam would feed me indefinitely. We could run out of money before we hit another meal like this one, or she could get tired of our routine, if not me.

When we finished eating, she made it clear that, far from getting tired of me, she had ideas, ideas that couldn't wait.

"I'm not doing this just for you, so you can forget about having any say in it."

"As long as I don't have to swim, what do I care?"

There was no use resisting. As compact as she was, Miriam had a right to somebody without flab. Besides, I wanted to see what it would take to make me look like the poster boy, and because swimming muscles weren't the kind that drew attention to themselves, I figured it was only a matter of not eating bad food. But it didn't stop there.

We made a deal, not much different from a duel. She challenged me to match the poster, so it was up to me to choose the weapon — no, exercise — to do the trick. I figured it couldn't be that bad, and went for the bicycle. Besides, a little exercise wasn't the same as training for competition. And anyway, life on the road made the whole plan unworkable, as long as she refused to learn to drive. To put her plans for me in motion, we'd have to settle down, so I thought I was home free, but there was another plan she hadn't forgot: the track.

Right after breakfast, while others went shopping for Thanksgiving turkeys and Christmas presents, Miriam bought a racing form, and it didn't matter that Oaklawn Park was dark until spring. Quicker than a photo flash, she made the leap from horses, and although it made a few thousand dollars seem like a lot more money, I didn't see how anyone could think the two sports were interchangeable.

"A turf club's a turf club, a trifecta's a trifecta, pace makes the race, and you can't beat the rail."

"You don't even like dogs."

"Better not to have what you like fuck up your business."

I couldn't believe how easy it was, like buying a gun with a fake ID. We drove to the track, proved that we weren't criminals by saying so, and they registered us as owners. For trainers, Miriam didn't want the ones with the most wins or even with the best win percentages. She went for someone innocuous, called him up and said she wanted to buy some dogs, we met him, and, because he didn't seem like a total jerk to her nor she to him, they negotiated a downpayment on four dogs and a month's upkeep. The dogs would still live in his kennel and race when he thought they should, so it was like he got cash for nothing. Money won by Miriam's dogs would be hers, but the purses couldn't meet the vet bills. Miriam let him know that she intended to clean up at the windows with inside tips she got from him, and he wouldn't deny this was possible.

C. Braxton Glade said, "A lot of owners want to change things overnight, so they bring in extra fancy sweaters for the hounds, like they know what they're doing, but they don't. A greyhound's not a fine-tuned machine, it's flesh and blood. You don't mess with the cooling system."

"We don't care what you do," she said. "Angel dust makes no difference to us, and if you want to sandbag 'em so they drop in grade, we don't mind."

"Althea's Red Zip, maiden two-year-old bitch," he said like he hadn't heard her. "Lean and hungry, nothing but an athlete."

"You know, Chick here was an athlete, but not like that."

"You don't say," he said, clearly not giving a shit.

I liked not telling him something that would have made his day a little more interesting.

"Do Do Daddy, 76 pounds, ungraded," he went on. "Don't pet him."

The dogs lived in stalls not much bigger than cages. Instead of straw on the floor, they had mattresses to curl up on, a couple of dishes for water and food, and a bag hung over each stall out of reach, trailing an unhooked I-V. When I asked C.B. about the medicine, he said you couldn't be too careful.

"Greyhounds ain't like other dogs."

I wasn't going to say it, but they looked like a cross between a basketball player and a rat.

"What I mean is, you can't operate on them. The

anesthetic can kill them."

The next one looked dead enough to fool the flies, but C.B. introduced him no differently, except to add, "He's my stud. His poppa was a monster, broke 30 in the 550, and when he hit the line, nobody else was in the picture. Blitzen, ungraded."

"So C.B. honey, how come none of these dogs have won shit?" she said. "Maiden, ungraded, ungraded — gimme a break! You didn't take 32 out of 187 races with these tailchasers."

"Grade A bitch, If You See Kay, 57 pounds, 7-for-12 lifetime, 29.92 in the 550, track record: you can't have the best if you don't take the rest."

She was alert, quiet, friendly, not a wagger but a snorter. Miriam put out her hand and If You See Kay sniffed, then licked, and I knew there'd be no more talk of sandbagging. When C.B. said she'd be racing tomorrow, he didn't have to add that she'd be an odds-on favorite.

"You can't tell her not to win. Not even an owner can do that."

Miriam didn't know what to think about owning a champion racing dog. That night she paced as much as was possible in our motel room, smoking cigarettes and drinking whiskey without ice. If You See Kay would have to break a leg not to win, at such measly odds that no quinella would reach double digits.

Althea's Red Zip and Do Do Daddy were also on the card, filling 8-dog fields in a maiden race and an ungraded race, where each figured to finish last. At least the feature's purse wasn't bad, but there was no way to make money betting on If You See Kay without guessing who would finish second. Filling quinellas with prohibitive favorites wasn't Miriam's idea of a good time, and trifectas were shell games for peanuts when chalk led the parade.

"To think I paid for this," she said, unable to hide that somehow, this was fun. She had expected to land a half-assed Grade B animal with a reasonably unpredictable form cycle who'd tank it as the favorite and pay boxcars when no one was looking, but C. Braxton Glade had sold her a dream.

I couldn't guess how Miriam knew so much about dog racing. We never had made it to the dogs in Portland. I had never been to them anywhere, and figured you only had to translate from horses. Miriam seemed to have a special feel for the game, though, so I didn't think I'd get away with translating from horses to dogs indefinitely.

One difference was, in dog racing you couldn't dump an animal into a lower class race to get an easy win. A dog dropped not because his handlers dropped him but because he didn't win enough at the higher level. Win, you move up; don't win, you move down. Drugs could always make a difference, but it was a mistake for Miriam to pop off about dope right out of the gate, even if she was only doing it, as she said, to test him.

A knock on the door brought chicken in a bag that wasn't so soaked with grease that you could see through it, and a hot-off-the-press racing form.

"Compliments of the Notel Motel," said the manager, Mrs. Black.

In the first race, Althea's Red Zip was number 7, with C.B. Glade, listed as trainer, and none other than M. Shifflet down as owner. The fourth race also listed her as the owner of Do Do Daddy, but not the twelfth and feature. Without asking, she put some money "for

me" into her enterprise and put down the owner of If
You See Kay as Olympic Kennel.

The I.O.C. wasn't going to like this. Riparian Park
wasn't Saratoga, but they'd find out. When they did, we
could say I had no part of it, but they'd still be pissed to
have their holy name tacked onto a greyhound syndi-
cate.

Mrs. Black wouldn't leave until we gave her a tip,
but there were no secrets. If You See Kay was a lock and
the nonwinners were losers. Nevertheless, she felt
proud to have dog people as guests.

"Anything I can do for you, don't hesitate to ask,"
she said.

"No Chick!" Miriam slapped my hand away from
the grease bag and explained I was on a diet. "If it's not
too much trouble, could you bring him some fruit?"

We woke up the next morning without knowing what to
wear. If You See Kay's style was speed on the lead, so
Miriam picked out a skin-tight red jump suit, but
because this was the feature race, her red was a classy
burgundy, flaunting an unbroken pattern of rhinestone
studded leg stripes. I thought we'd have to go to every
store in Billyville, Arkansas, before finding the right outfit to go with hers, but the string tie with a fake ruby,
the black jacket, and pink shirt couldn't have been a
better match. The lady at Goodwill swore it wouldn't
look out of place at the track.

"Only a real man can wear pink," said Miriam, and
I couldn't help wondering whose clothes these had
been. Dog punters gone broke could make togs like
these no more personalized than prom rentals.

Nobody cared what you wore at the track. Even in
the turf club, where they had a sports jacket dress code,

they weren't too proud to hand out the stained seersuckers to guys arriving in T-shirts.

When we finally arrived at the turf club, I noticed something else that set it apart from the grandstand: down in the pit, all was bare linoleum, unpainted cinderblocks, and uncushioned benches, but up here, no surface wasn't padded. With blue carpet running up the walls and around the ceiling, smells never left the turf club, they just shuffled around. Cigars, perfume, sweat, money, cigarettes, fried shrimp, fried steak, and booze blended, separated, and recombined, no matter how many cans of Mountain Mist, Sea Spray, and Pine Barren they sprayed. Vent fans sucked what they could and left behind a drone that, like the air, never cleared. A race would be finishing, with everyone going crazy below, and up in the turf club it was like you weren't there.

Upstairs and down, the walls had pictures of winning dogs in the cluster of shots from the race and afterwards with their owners and trainers – no different from winning horse photos. Would anyone who saw me on the wall with If You See Kay at Riparian Park connect me to the Hog Springs poster when I didn't look anything like I did here? The photos were no more varied than a wallpaper pattern, but then we saw Leadout to Victory.

Leadout to Victory was a display you couldn't ignore, on a wall that faced you as you stood to bet. It honored the leadouts, old teenagers or young adults who walked the dogs in the post parade, by showing them after they worked here, and to survey Leadout to Victory was to see nobody who hadn't made it big. They weren't "just" druggists and insurance salesmen, beauticians and sheriffs. One owned a chain of drug stores, another ran an insurance company, three were fashion models, and no politician on the wall was anything lower than a U.S. Representative. You would have thought the road to success led not through Lawrenceville and Princeton, but Riparian Park and Catfish Community College.

The Friday before Thanksgiving a special Turkey Trifecta pulled people out of nowhere, filling the stands with gobbling lunatics. Even upstairs, the owners, trainers, and high rollers couldn't stop talking about the challenge of picking the order of finish of the bottom three dogs of any race. And it wasn't just turkeys that were the prizes, but pre-basted, hormone-laced, MSG-seasoned Biggie Buttered Beauties.

"You're not going to try? We have no place to put it," I said, but Miriam wanted to get into the spirit, especially since our dog had to finish in the bottom trio of the first race.

She worked so hard on her bottom three picks, she almost didn't get to make a regular bet. She wasn't alone. Bettors rushed from the entry boxes surrounding the big plastic case holding dozens of frozen turkeys to get in line at the windows, so the track had to move back post time another five minutes, or not enough money would be bet to cover all of the daily doubles. Some unlikely combos were paying infinity-to-one.

"Chick, cover the orphan doubles, you never know."

I did, because you can't afford to miss easy money, even if it meant taking impossible chances. Nobody was into contrary betting like we were. It wasn't hard to see which combos had been left untouched, only hard to bring myself to bet on Althea's Red Zip.

"If she doesn't win, I hope she loses," I flashed my tickets to C.B. and Miriam.

C.B. said he only had her in the turkey trot, so Miriam didn't show him her serious bet: $100 to show on Althea's Red Zip.

"It's not too late to cancel," I said.

"Cancel schmancel: she don't show, she don't eat."

Heads turned, glasses raised, and nobody didn't gobble.

An unscratched recording of the whistle march from *Bridge Over the River Kwai* came and went with the dogs. I was too busy watching the leadouts to study how Althea's Red Zip looked, as I tried to pick the models from the vice-presidents among the five boys and three girls when suddenly I saw our mistake.

"You didn't notice?" I whispered to Miriam, who refused to talk below a shout.

"Notice what — that we can't lose?"

"What the leadouts are wearing," I said, but it wasn't something she should have wanted to accept.

Some tracks decked out their leadouts like third world admirals, while others had them wear no more than overalls. No wonder Miriam's jump suit went so well with my pink shirt.

The dogs were in the gate, which wasn't a gate but a row of cages with metal floors wired to shock the dogs into action. The lights reversed, setting the track aglow against the darkened stands, and the cages popped open to a bell as the tote machines shut off, but then, unlike the ponies, there was hardly any noise. The course was so small and the race so fast that the announcer gave no call beyond, "They're off!" Until the mumble grew into a moan from below, all you heard was the whir of an unreal giant bone zipping ahead of the field, and barking.

Like most of the races, this one began on the stretch turn, which pushed dogs like our number 7 wide out of the gate, but Miriam didn't fret when they went by the first time. The co-favorite led, as Althea's Red Zip avoided the scramble in mid-pack and had no trouble moving up on the straightaway. The leader had the clubhouse turn to himself and cruised down the backstretch, with the field strung out so you could tell them apart by color, if not number. By the final turn, he had company, forcing a picture to call the winner, while it was unexpected yet obvious how effortlessly Althea's Red Zip took third.

Even if she hadn't cannonballed into the show pool, Miriam's 20-1 shot wasn't going to pay much, with a 5-2 and a 4-1 finishing one, two. The big groan came from the fact that the other 5-2 favorite finished dead last, which undid so many Turkey Trifectas that hardly a gobble sounded.

"The bitch did it," Miriam waved her ticket like it wasn't the stupidest bet ever.

"Don't get your hopes up," I said, "we spent fifty bucks adopting those orphans."

Then, like magic, we were even, with Althea's Red Zip paying $3.00 to show, recovering the $50, not to mention a piece of the purse.

"No guts, no glory," said Miriam.

It didn't matter what we wore. For the next fifteen minutes, nobody could say we didn't know our dogs.

The wake-up call came despite the DO NOT DISTURB sign, and I hit the road, humping a 3-speed from oat bran to fresh fruit, to sweat off the surf-n-turf we had to celebrate If You See Kay's win. Luck couldn't explain Miriam's feel for the dogs any more than C. Braxton Glade would explain why he had cut us in on a winner like that, but money took care of any worries. As long as the windows gave more than they took away and the purses fed the dogs, I couldn't care how it was that Glade needed a sudden shot of cash. It bothered me more that Miriam wouldn't go into her dog track past.

"I can't help it, it's in the blood," was as far as she

went, while I covered what she might have said with every mile.

You didn't notice how hilly a place was until you rode a bicycle. At first, even as cold as it was, I would get soaked, but after a few days I inevitably sweat less and got sore more. Then something happened that I hadn't counted on: the body took over. Harder rides up steeper hills in higher gears kept me on the road so long, Miriam asked if it wasn't too much.

"Can't you take it easy?"

"Not unless I stop. Either I do it or I don't: poster boy or dough boy, take your pick."

She picked dogs, going back over the result charts and past performances to uncover form cycles and key races and anticipate the effect of post position changes. I figured her new game would fade like any fad without me getting involved, but for a whole week the losses didn't offset the wins, and then she bought a stopwatch.

Our greyhound racing forms didn't mention pace, and Miriam was positive that nothing tipped a key race as much as a tough pace. Before, if two or three dogs came out of a particular race to win their next times out, she would follow other dogs from that race and cover them, no matter where they popped up. Now, with her stopwatch to break the races into segments, she didn't have to wait for any dogs to win without her. No dog exiting a fast-paced race failed to draw her action. She called it a method, not a system, and said it couldn't lose. Fluke or science, her homework paid off better than a job, so like it or not, we were set.

I didn't like it. Maybe I wouldn't like it anywhere. Hadn't the story of my life been a move from one place to the next, with each destination turning out to be a little worse than the one before it? Miriam had her handicapping, but my own self-improvement project made less sense to me the more I did it, because getting into shape made the reason for getting into shape disappear. Then once you were back in shape, there was nothing to do but fall out of shape, and so the process could repeat indefinitely until you quit or died or came to some meaningless point of arrival.

I had no place to go, just an itch to leave. No, that's wrong. From the start, I'd known where we were headed, and even if we had to turn around and come back to some town along the way, we couldn't stop until we ran out of road.

Dog season didn't last forever. Around here, it didn't go past Christmas. All the planning she did on the coming races left Miriam no time to talk about what we would do next. While riding the bike, I made up conversations with her that came out as the lines country and western singers sang when they pretended to be dissatisfied husbands or wives ("Why don't you love me like you used to do?") in songs Mrs. Black played and Miriam didn't mind while she went through the past performances and I ate fruit.

Mrs. Black didn't like me. My past cut no ice with this woman whose husband ran off with a teenager and whose teenage son had been killed in the army. To her, Miriam was the brains of the outfit and I was no more than a dildo licensed to drive. I tried to talk to her, but these conversations didn't break down her resistance so much as put her on guard. When I asked what her husband did for a living she said that he was just like me: he didn't do squat.

"He played the dogs, didn't he?"

"Pussy was his game," she said and I didn't push it.

Our conversations never became arguments and served mostly as room dividers, the way running water or a radio makes private space in a small room. With me alone in the room, Miriam might have had to talk; without me, she was free to think.

At the track, I was her caddy, sent to cover the orphans and mop up the slop in a flurry of busywork that kept me from distracting her from her real bets, which were so complicated, she couldn't trust me to make them. The difference between a triple key wheel and a triple key box couldn't wait to be discovered after it was too late to change. She asked me for advice, but didn't take it. She thanked me for not bothering her, and finally put me in charge of stopping the watch.

If You See Kay kept winning and none of the other dogs hit the board. I lost twenty pounds and nobody noticed, except for Mrs. Black, who said it was proof that I was up to no good. Miriam won and lost and told no one how well or badly she was doing overall, because that was something you could never tell, even if it seemed to show. Altogether, it wasn't an awful routine, but then C.B. Glade took his family to breakfast at Hog Springs, and when he came to call, the routine was no longer enough.

He said we couldn't end the race meeting without doing something special, and so we met with Beau Merle, general manager of Riparian Park. Merle bought us drinks in the turf club, even though the races were on and there was no way Miriam could gamble and I could keep time while drinking, but rather than object, Miriam announced her retirement.

Glade didn't blink, but this was the first I heard that we weren't going to follow the dogs to Southland. Didn't he wonder what she intended to do with the kennel? After all, he had said more than once that Riparian was no more than a training session for Southland, and had even scratched If You See Kay from the Getaway Day Handicap to give her some time off to prepare for that meet. Soon greyhounds from Florida, Oregon, Arizona, Vermont, Colorado, Iowa, and everywhere else the lure led the pack would go to West Memphis, Arkansas, for the unprecedented Challenge of Champions. It wasn't a positive sign that Riparian Park's ace handicapper was selling her dog short of the big race, the dream of triumph C.B. Glade had described as the Kentucky Derby, Breeders Cup Classic, and Travers Stakes rolled into one.

Merle wore a banker's suit, we had turned in our leadout uniforms for clothes that weren't ridiculous, and C.B. had on the snazziest coat from his closet.

"I am proud, as an American and as a man, to have met you," Merle began, and by the way he wouldn't let go of my hand, I knew we were in for the works.

Never mind that this was Miriam's show, that it had been her idea to set up shop here, that she was the one who succeeded at a game where nearly everyone failed. He was after me, not her. And although it was kind of embarrassing to have him fawning over me instead of her, I couldn't deny that I liked how my medals still had clout.

"It would be a shame if we didn't show our appreciation for all you have done to bring a world class act to Billyville, and so permit me to arrange a ceremony in your honor."

Before I could say, why bother, Miriam said, why not?

Another race went off without our bets, but out of some sort of respect, everyone stopped talking in order to watch.

"Not only would we like you to be the honorary stewards of Getaway Day, we'll change the name of the Getaway Day Handicap to the Olympic Stakes."

"Oh boy, Chick, can't you see it? We could hold hands like champs on the stand, wearing nothing but bathing suits."

"Not again."

Merle cleared his throat and didn't speak. Maybe he and Miriam didn't share the same view of "world class."

"I don't think we should drag the Olympics into this," I said. "Not directly. It wouldn't be in good taste."

Nobody laughed.

"I used to do this kind of work, so if you like, I'll put something together that won't bend the card out of shape. Some fanfare, an announcement, no more than a few words."

Beau Merle was in no mood to let me run his show. Not that I wanted to. I only made the offer so Miriam wouldn't run wild.

"And we can't leave out C.B.," I said, "let's give him an award," which must have sounded more like an insult than a compliment.

"Yeah, C.B., how about if we clone a medal for you, a nice brassy gold on a red, white, and blue ribbon," said Miriam, not kidding.

Not kidded, Glade smiled.

"You're right," said Merle, "it can't be too much like the Olympics. That would be inappropriate. Your input has been invaluable, Mr. Honochick. Yessir, there's no disputing taste. Nothing can't be in good taste."

He bought another round and said he would take care of it, and that we wouldn't be disappointed.

More races went off and we sat watching so passively that it seemed not like a night of dog races but a nightclub with a monotonous floor show.

"What's this about you not going to Southland?" said C.B.

She shrugged and said something I couldn't hear, which must have had something to do with giving him a deal on the dogs, because he bought the next round. We didn't pay much attention to the feature, other than to wonder what the pace was, and watched the odds change.

The tote board was just pretty if you didn't care what it meant. Bright blue amounts rippled into new figures every few moments under flashing red ratios, with a yellow dot making fractions in the dark over the glow of the dirt, as if Riparian Park had no purpose other than to look nice and make people happy.

"You know, I never got to go to the track with my uncle," she said, "but he showed me everything, the son of a bitch. I helped him keep records and he covered my action, but he said you couldn't hope for much in the long run."

C.B. nodded and studied the post parade, but I couldn't let this go by.

"Where was this and how old were you and were you living with him and not your parents or on vacation?"

"In Florida I wasn't old enough."

Even a thank-you ceremony in good taste didn't seem like a good reason to stay an extra week, especially if we weren't going to keep riding or letting it ride. For a couple of drifters these folks would never see again, we got lots of attention, what with Christmas parties happening every night. Before the parties could make a total wreck of us, we went back to Hog Springs for breakfast, and I stood as Miriam demanded, with that poster look I couldn't ruin with a smirk — not the anthem glaze but a look from before, full of hunger, desire, determination, and confidence.

Arkansas did more for us than we expected, but I hadn't expected Miriam to change her mind about New Orleans. She didn't explain her change any more than she explained what she'd said about her uncle. I knew not to bug her with questions. No amount of questions had made any difference before. And now, more than any sense of dread or adventure, Miriam seemed charged up with an irrepressible need to take on what she had left behind. She was suddenly more eager to leave than I was, but we couldn't until we finished our gig at Riparian Park.

An outsider might not understand what it meant to be named honorary stewards at Getaway Day of a dog track. As we stood in the dinky infield, we couldn't make out what the PA said through the wall of light. Beau Merle and C.B. were with us, and when the announcer stopped droning, the anthem came on and nobody had to say what to do. Luckily, the field mike wasn't working, so we spared the crowd any speeches. C.B. and Miriam accepted plaques from Merle and for some unaccountable reason, we all bowed when we shook hands. Maybe gestures had to be magnified so the crowd wouldn't miss what we were supposed to be doing.

The funny thing was, even a real steward didn't have a lot to do at the dog track. Without jockeys, there were no fouls to call, so aside from monitoring drug tests, they did little more than we did.

We had surf-n-turf one more time and didn't drink too much, which was a good thing, because our stint as honorary stewards didn't end with a pre-race ceremony.

After the last race, Beau Merle led us back to the winner's circle and there with the track photographer were the eight of them, five boys in the pink frilly shirts and black cutaway coats, three girls in the burgundy jump suits, the promise of Billyville, Arkansas, the leaders of tomorrow/the leadouts of today, and when they greeted us, smiling and shaking our hands, they didn't have to add that we'd be going up on the wall of Leadout to Victory.

-1

We needed a place to stay, but the hotels in our price range weren't the kind you went to unless you were alone, and we knew better than to try our luck in the city parks of this town. Christmas week was too close to the Sugar Bowl to rely on fair rates from the non-dives. Not that we followed football.

What we wound up doing wasn't much different from what you'd expect from a typical couple on vacation.

"Chick, we're not going to do *that*."

"No vacancy for less than a hundred a night."

That was the New Orleans phone book, and there was no use pretending that it wasn't a valuable resource. After the ghost town, the dog track had given us the taste of the good life, so I wasn't going to settle for a slum. I didn't need a most livable city or a tropical paradise, just a $100 room without the cost. The answer was Southern Hospitality; the question was, don't you remember me?

It took no more than a sink bath in a gas station rest room to make us look passable. Nevertheless, Miriam had her doubts about trading on old friendships for places to stay. She didn't feel up to the culture clash.

"If it doesn't feel right, we won't stay, we'll make some excuse and go," I said.

"One excuse after another, and they'll suck it up without a sneer. Then, when we're off to bed, they'll gloat over how you didn't make it like they did. Come off it, nothing we do changes the way we are. We could switch clothes, wash the car, wash our clothes, trade the car, and still something about us wouldn't smell right. You'll never guess who came begging for a bed, they'll say."

"You don't understand. We'll have to beg not to stay with them. There's nothing these people hate more than having you refuse an invitation. Wasn't it like that when you were here?"

"I never lived here, and when I passed through, I didn't associate with the people from the swank side of town. You generally didn't see them puking from bar to bar with their pom-poms hanging out. You really didn't see those people, either. All you ever really see is that it doesn't matter where you're from: money insulates everyone. They're invincible. And you're untouchable."

"Just because a name comes with a swank address doesn't mean everything's rosy. It may look like the good life, but it can't be that good, especially if they have kids. When nobody's looking, the kids fuck the hired help. I'll bet there isn't a parent in the phone book who wouldn't trade places with us."

"Then what's to make us trade places with them, even for no more than a night?"

"Because it doesn't stop at the room. You can't turn down a shot at a great dinner, with unlimited booze. In this town, you're nowhere unless you're up, on, and over."

"Don't you mean down and out?"

All around us were people you weren't surprised to find away from the office at this time of day. After driving all night and sleeping most of the morning, we hadn't arrived in time for happy hour at Manny Lagoon's. We had a table in the courtyard, next to the mercifully unused ping-pong table, across from some junkies who ate doughnuts and drank chocolate milk. The junkies didn't bother us, and we returned the favor. Nobody had the energy to be a jerk.

They couldn't all be junkies: some were drunks and others were college boys out for experience. They didn't talk much, but when they did it came in that weird accent that sounded more from Brooklyn than the South. Come to think of it, they didn't sound much different from Miriam.

"You sure you didn't live here?"

"I decided not to," she said.

"You sure you don't want to leave?"

"Not until I ask some rich kid how he likes the maid. Don't let me stop you from picking a name. I can't wait to check out the help. Tell me, Jeeves, do we undress for dinner or is it come-as-you-are. Bet you can't pick a name that doesn't have a swimming pool."

She talked me out of it and dared me into it, but there was a chance nobody would be home. Call a few numbers and get on with our lives — no problem. But it was only a few days before Christmas, and not only were they home, they were primed to be generous. The first number hit pay dirt, and the guy wasted no time inviting us.

"We could not show up," I said.

"Please, I wouldn't miss this for anything."

"They don't expect us until afternoon. You weren't planning on staying here until then, were you? We could, but what I mean is, if you really don't want to, we won't."

"Won't we? Well, we wouldn't be re-living the glory days of college like those slummers over there, would we? Don't tell me, this guy's a fraternity brother, your leader in the baby elephant walk."

I wasn't in a fraternity, but I knew what she meant. Although a daisy chain of college boys, each connected to the other by an ever-more-shortened line from around the balls of the one in front to the neck of the one in back had nothing to do with me and Artie Gifford, Miriam resented my old school ties. They showed privileges, advantages she never had, a life I rejected. Did she resent my rejection more than the fact that I had advantages that were unavailable to her?

"Look, when I was in college, I did nothing but swim and study."

"Aw Chick, I didn't mean — "

"I spent two years at Crescent University, one in a dorm and one in an apartment; then after Munich, it made no sense to finish. You couldn't say it was a waste of time, though. College didn't keep me from anything I wouldn't have done otherwise. It's not like I have regrets."

To make her feel better, I said Artie Gifford wasn't like me. He wasn't a jock; he was just a guy from my floor who liked to get high. I went to Crescent for the swim team, for a coach who practically guaranteed me a shot at the Olympics, and Gifford went there because it was the only decent school his family could buy his way into where he probably wouldn't flunk out. He came from a family of achievers, men and women who were not only all lawyers but intellectuals who spoke at least three languages fluently, while I came from a family of coasters, where the guys slipped into marriages with bosses' daughters and the gals got knocked up by chance.

"Don't worry, when I last saw him, he was such a mess, there's no way he could have lived up to the family standard."

"He lives where he lives, and he didn't get there by blowing dope."

Miriam froze and I couldn't blame her. Like most adults the world over, she couldn't care less about Christmas, but the tears she could disguise as sentiment rather than grief. After all, the Giffords had welcomed us as family for the biggest family day of the year, even though Artie and I hadn't been in touch since college. It would have been ungrateful to let on that something was wrong.

"Don't worry," I said, "they like us."

"We haven't got any presents for them. Not that they should want any, after that stupid house gift. It's going to be like one of those dreams where you find yourself in line at the supermarket with nothing on."

How were we to know that they would have four perfect kids who, aside from being unperturbed by sex or drugs, were as kind and considerate as the parents? You couldn't tell Miriam that her worst fears wouldn't come true, that each of them would give presents to us.

"We'll make something," I said, going through the litter in our baggage to find no more than match books, dog racing programs, and dead tote tickets.

"There isn't time."

It was nearly mid-morning and we were holding everything up because, Maysie Gifford explained, in this family you didn't raid the presents by yourself until everyone was ready. At age seven she was wise enough not to be impatient.

"Too bad it's not Halloween," I said. "We could go as the unswept floor of a racetrack."

"Give up, Chick, we have nothing anyone would want."

"Oh no? I've got something and I'll give it for both of us, even though I vowed never to do it again. Swimming lessons, none other than the old Reno marineland gig."

"They'll be embarrassed and it wouldn't be from me. This was a terrible idea — not because of them. We're the stinkers: not you, me."

She fell back crying, so I answered the door, where Patricia, age ten, reminded us that it wouldn't be long before breakfast.

The carpet and walls were too thick to leak sound, and we had been given a suite of rooms that uncoiled from the main house to encircle the pool on three sides. When Artie did his laps, I screened him out by turning on TV, but my refusal to join him or even to get wet couldn't go unexplained much longer.

"We don't owe them anything but to be nice guests," I said.

"Any other time of year we could take them all out to eat, but not tonight. Tonight it's nothing but family and friends, and the next night it'll be more friends. I've never felt so worthless."

She had a point, but didn't want me to agree.

"It's a big family, nobody's going to keep score on presents," I said.

"Fuck it," she yanked on her jeans without finding her panties, "time to be nice again."

Although their home had double-high ceilings and archways, chandeliers, columned porch, and plenty of rooms, they kept it so spotless that the air was free of must. Our string of rooms resembled a modern hotel suite, but in the main house the rooms got bigger and older and more full of antiques, old portraits, and stuff you wouldn't expect a family with kids to keep from destroying. On top of it all was Christmas, with pine boughs, ribbons, gold and red sashes, and giant glass balls arranged around every mantle and window so that it was impossible to look or sniff anywhere and not hear a choir of carolers. The green wall-to-wall carpet gave the white woodwork a Christmas look in any season, Artie's wife Susan said when we told her how the house impressed us, as if her feats of decorating were effortless.

Susan Gifford didn't reassure Miriam, through no fault of her own. She was small and beautiful, with chiseled features, and the cut of her clothes wasn't so domestic that a guy didn't want to keep looking at her. She held your eyes with her eyes, kept you from straying with a command of diverse subjects that made us feel dumpy and unsophisticated. I told Miriam I was much better off with her than with anyone like Susan Gifford, but I had nothing to do with it.

Susan's greeting made sleeping in Christmas morning no cause for apology. She and the girls were at the table while Artie and the fifteen-year-old twins made breakfast, but that didn't stop Frank, the blond twin, from rushing to help Miriam with her chair. Frank and Denny didn't deviate from the rest of the family. They were chipper, polite, and handsome, but unlike Maysie, they were too big to get away with crawling on us in the jungle game.

"Not at the table," the mother stopped her before she could go into that routine where she was the monkey and we were trees.

This wasn't your Hog Springs pig-a-thon, but it was just as spectacular. Now a partner in a law firm rivaling his father's, Artie said no accomplishment made him prouder than mastering hollandaise. Instead of the homemade mess you might expect from someone slapping together poached eggs, ham, muffins, and sauce like he'd had in a restaurant, his Eggs Benedict were as good as any I'd had when the agency paid the tab: oblong dimpleless golf balls that bled to blend smoothly with the sauce when you cut them. As for the hollandaise sauce, I was nobody to tell the difference between the canned and the real, but if this was canned, it was better than real.

The Champagne was incredibly rich, like toasted bagels with butter and honey, trailing off in a twinkle that made you pinch yourself at such an impossible combo of the light and the full. And the French roast took no prisoners. Minus the chicory, it could have been Seattle coffee.

The kids went through their stockings at the table, so there was no pressure to make conversation. We said how great the food was and the kids shared their haul, even though the haul wasn't candy but make-up. They got goofy, and between dares and bluffs, the boys and Artie didn't quit until they put on make-up, too.

I concentrated on the food and Miriam made no move for the compacts, lipsticks, and eye shadows. Together we sat sucking some pleasure from chunks of non-sweet white chocolate while the Giffords took turns outdoing each other. From the way they dawdled, you would have thought there were no more goodies. Was this a family that didn't buy real presents but instead made donations to charity in each other's names?

"I don't get it," I said. "How can you stand not to rush the loot?"

"Wouldn't you like to know," said Patricia.

Denny, the twin whose hair wasn't blond, cleared the table while Frank worked the sink.

"We've learned to savor the moment," said Susan, "because if you rush, you don't enjoy it as much."

"Christmas is a religious day for us," said Artie, "even though we're not, strictly speaking, religious. We have our rituals, and if we don't do them a certain way, it feels less like Christmas."

Pancaked up to the yin-yang, the patriarch couldn't resist a peek in the compact mirror.

Denny returned and nodded to his parents while we still heard Frank in the kitchen, which didn't account for the sounds on the other side of the dining room doors. With a toot, a muffled cymbal, and a clearing of throats, the house not only seemed mysteriously full of people but on the verge of something the family obviously expected. The guys made no move to take off their make-up.

Unseen hands drew open the sliding doors to the downbeat of a brassy Christmas tune. The daughters seemed to float forward, with the twins and parents filling in behind them, and everyone reflected these unreal smiles that were seared by the blaze of light. Artie and Susan turned their smiles on us, each offering us an arm, and we had no choice.

"Come on," I whispered, "we can't be bad guests."

"No shit."

Not one but two cameras flanked us in the foyer, the hand-held scooting ahead while a dolly swooped around to hit us with a reverse angle. Nobody had told us not to look at the cameras, so Miriam and I stared at the crew while some guy with a clipboard maneuvered to point at this present or that. We weren't the stars. First Maysie and then Patricia fell to her knees and squealed as she ripped open a package and the camera zoomed in for reactions and sighs, laughter and the moans of others, who didn't scream all at once.

It was a Barbie and a Barbie miniature movie set, with full costume closet and plenty of back lot scenery that was going to take days to put together, no matter what movie they chose: western or cop, monster or romance.

I had been so distracted by the director, cameras, and lights of our set, that only then did I notice the big picture, the unsurpassed splendor of the tree and all the presents. I wasn't the only one taken by surprise.

Miriam bellowed, "I can't believe this shit."

"Watch it, you don't want Barbie to wind up on the cutting room floor."

Nobody stopped the action. No doubt careful to avoid the shot, the director waddled our way while he scribbled something on a pad he shoved at us. We didn't have to read it to know what it said: Act natural, but keep it clean!

"Goll-eey," Frank virtually sang, "not an electric football game! Gee, thanks, Dad, or no," he turned to the camera, "Grandpa, it's just what I've always wanted. Come on, Denny, you be the Saints and I'll be the 49ers," he held it for his twin to see, but not grab.

"Oh no," said Denny, "you be the Saints and I'll be the 49ers."

Others laughed like they got the joke, but maybe no crack could fail to get a rise out of them.

The kids got through a few rounds, each managing to upstage the others by blowing and sucking the oohs and ahs before Susan and Artie unwrapped token packages: ski sweater and waterproof watch. Instead of tokens of nothing, these proved to be theme presents, with the watch leading a parade of swim fins, Bermuda shorts, and sunglasses that inevitably came to an envelope of airline tickets, while the sweater led to goggles, gloves, and an envelope of its own.

After a mock wrangling of where to go, they said in unison: "I know, why not go both places?"

No package was received without a word for Grandpa, even stuff given from one of them to another ("Gee Grandpa, isn't this a lovely dress?"). The Giffords didn't just smile for show — they liked being on camera. I guess this applied to many people who hadn't been burned out by the promo circuit.

Forty minutes into this orgy of greed, where the silliest gifts were clues for prizes nobody would trade for whatever came from behind door number three, Miriam and I were still getting used to it. Any fear that we hadn't done our part was long gone. We had paid them back simply by not telling Grandpa to fuck off. Was there no limit to their love for the lens?

No such luck. As if on cue, the family bunched around, with the girls at our knees and the boys beaming upward, while the parents flanked us and the cameras zoomed in, so our only consolation was that, without make-up, we must have looked like zombies. The brass went from "Hark the Herald Angels Sing" to a toney and subdued "America the Beautiful," and as the microphone lowered, I got the uneasy feeling that they were going to sing.

They didn't sing; they hummed.

"Grandpa," said Artie, like he was addressing not an old man but a crowd of preschoolers, "you know, the best part of Christmas isn't the glitter or even the wonderful presents, but the spirit of goodwill, friendship, and love we feel for one another. And not just feel! This is the time of year we express our love in ways we can't at other times. Once more, Grandpa, words alone can't express our gratitude, so on this special occasion we have for you a special surprise."

He paused and the musicians veered into an

unflawed knock-off of the Olympic theme.

"Grandpa, I don't know if you remember, but this is Ken Honochick and his lovely wife, Miriam," said Susan. "We haven't seen them in ages, but they took time out of their busy holiday schedule to renew an old, dear friendship."

"Munich, Germany, 1972," said Artie, "now you remember, don't you? Yes, the Olympics nobody will ever forget, and here's the fellow who annihilated the competition in the backstroke, winning both gold medals: Ken Honochick, champion."

What did it matter that I had no speech? Behind the camera in front stood a guy with a stack of idiot cards, and the music tailed off so I couldn't ignore him.

"Thank you, Artie, Susan, Denny and Frank, Patricia and Maysie," I read like I'd caught the disease, "and Grandpa, thank you for helping to make this Christmas one of the best I've ever had, although, ha ha, it hasn't been a white Christmas."

"White Christmas?" everyone said, even if there was no such card.

The intro sealed our fate, but in case Grandpa missed it, Patricia said, "Now I wouldn't say that... "

Maysie was the one who sang, and as she laid waste to the first verse, I hoped there wouldn't be a second. We had gone beyond the call of unselfish duty. They had their swag and the old fart had his indelible video Christmas Card. Cut it, print it, wrap it up, and break out the bourbon, but no, there was a second verse.

Maysie stepped forward, but before she could bleat another note, Miriam stepped to sing in front of her, and I hoped no more.

It was the Giffords' turn not to blame Miriam. There had been no warning of this command performance. Maybe they had sprung it on other guests without suffering any retaliation. Artie claimed he thought we would love it, and you honestly couldn't tell which he regretted more: offending us or mortifying his father-in-law.

You might have thought the kids would be relieved to pop the balloon, but no, they moped. For all we knew, the mansion belonged to Grandpa, and this business with the cameras was cheap rent, and so, worse than the shock that might stop his heart, Miriam's act could have been the shock to make him see how they patronized and abused him.

"Big deal: erase the end and nobody will be the wiser" I said.

"It wouldn't help," said Artie, "that was live."

While Susan rounded up the kids, he continued to apologize for the "misunderstanding." He said the rest of Christmas would be on TV as well, not having to dis-invite us to dinner. Neither did he bother to kick us out. We could use the guest house for a hotel room as long as we liked, or if we didn't want to stay, we could leave without saying goodbye.

The story on the invalid grandfather might have made sense to anyone whose life was ruled by sports on TV. He had produced sports telecasts, which made him not want to settle for tape delay. Not only that, he had made commercials. There was a chance that we knew each other or even that I had worked for him, which made me want to talk to him and not at him.

Artie excused himself to get ready for the next scene, in the room with the fire going while the family members took turns unloading what Christmas meant to each of them. This diversion gave us a chance to look at the tree with nobody to pester us.

Not only tall, but full and wide, it had short needles that were so dark, it could have been flown here yesterday. For all of the branches to decorate, there wasn't a single sprig without an ornament. None cheap. Antique balls and miniature scenes, ivory and ebony angels, manger figures with jewels for eyes, and lights that weren't the wimpy blinkers but the classic red, green, blue, yellow, orange, and violet bulbs rounded out like the shapes of mid-century cars made the tree prettier than a casino.

Although the Giffords had gone through a buzzsaw opening act, the presents hadn't been snatched away and the wrapping still glowed everywhere. Heavy foil in throbbing magentas, chartreuses, and cyans advertised just what you would expect from a family with so much money that it couldn't resist showing off on TV yet not so much money that it could.

"What do you bet there isn't some connection between their geezer and my ex-in-laws?"

"Geezer schmeezer, I say there is no Grandpa. If there was, he wouldn't have let me pull that stunt without getting on the horn. Like Artie says, it's all one big ritual that makes for Christmas and not Groundhog Day. Which reminds me, Christmas: you wouldn't stiff me now, would you, Chick?"

Back in the room we gave each other the best of all presents, and when she wrapped herself around me, it felt twice as good because I knew she wasn't sorry any more.

We had arrived here on the run, and the sanctuary of a big home and a happy family could have made us insecure. This slice of life was a free lunch I might have had and she never knew. We might have taken all we could from them without paying more than a parting shot, but we picked up and straightened everything, and didn't leave the bed unmade. Then I wrote a thank-you note, which she checked to make sure it didn't go too far, and we made our escape down a corridor filled with roast smells and canned laughter and outside to the city of Mardi Gras on a Christmas Night we took for New Year's Eve. Although the best restaurants would doubtlessly be closed, anything was better than crashing their dinner to be taken in by that audience of one while he was being fed by tubes.

It was balmy and humid, and as we loaded the car, we watched them through windows that had been sprayed with fake frost that framed them with an extra brightness for the invisible cameras. Once again, the singing started, singing destined not to be interrupted.

And yet for us, and for a few good people, "White Christmas" could never be the same.

Back in the French Quarter, we had no trouble finding that spot where a tourist might stop to spread out a map. She made me play the tourist, with a map of Florida instead of New Orleans, and I went along, with the map trembling as she went back twenty years, and when it didn't end, we celebrated.

Some joints never closed. My favorites were one on the Streetcar Named Desire line, with tiny blue and white check tiles covering the floor and a fourteen-foot alligator hanging from the ceiling, and the one that used to be divided into a bar for whites and a bar for nonwhites, and that nowadays was divided into a bar and a grocery. Guess which side didn't get stocked with dry goods?

Miriam wanted to know more about my time at Crescent University, then agreed that the college life of a swimmer wasn't much of a story.

"Didn't you ever do anything?"

"What does anyone do in college: study, learn how

to get fucked up without puking, try to get laid."

"You never got laid?"

"I don't remember," I lied.

"Oh, you southern belles, 'Ah cain't remember,' waking up naked in a bed full of fish, 'Ah trust y'all didn't besmirch mah honah.'"

"Yeah, I came, but I don't know where it went. She was tight and hairy, and we were clumsy and inexperienced. My dick was so scabbed, I thought she gave me the clap, but I shouldn't have said so."

"No, Mr. Tactful! Was it, 'Hey, bitch, you didn't give me the clap, did you?'? And she goes, 'Nah, that's what you get from jerking off on the toilet seat.'"

"She wanted nothing to do with a guy who doubted her purity. Or maybe it was more like, if I had something, who's to say I didn't catch it from someone else and then pass it to her. Like I said, we were both inexperienced. She didn't know enough to know that I knew even less."

"Not exactly, ignorance is bliss."

"More like blisters," I said, having more fun now just because then it hadn't been any fun at all, and wondering whether most people don't look back on sex in college the same way.

New Orleans wasn't your usual college town. I probably saw my parents more than ever, and it didn't bother me that I gave them a reason to come down here whenever they wanted. The old man was always getting transferred, and my mother had to keep up with the relocations, so if you threw in my nonstop training schedules, we hardly ever had a chance to sit down to dinner together, except when on vacation.

"Poor kid, bet you never went anywhere they didn't have an ocean or pool. Not the Caribbean, not Mexico, Greece, Tahiti."

"Sometimes the water wasn't easy to get used to, like the pool in Maryland with too much chlorine, or the one in Connecticut that was hotter than Atlanta, or the Keys where they kept the porpoise."

"Didn't it get old that all you did was swim?"

"Not just swim: win. I was the perfect son: clean, bright, unbeatable."

She wasn't teasing, but there was an edge to her rap that seemed calculated to draw attention.

"You too?" said a guy on another stool, "I used to be a musician," but he wouldn't say why he quit. "They thought I'd thrown my life away, but when I made it, they couldn't get over how great I was. Some say the high point was The Bitter End, or that night in Paris when Mingus bowed and gave me his stage, but I swear, none of it compared to watching Mama watch me on TV."

His friend was a lady who had lost her job after writing an exposé that won a Pulitzer, the prize not having as much clout as the ex-general who ran the mercenary training school she busted, and next to her was the guy who had invented the shopping cart, buying drinks for a former prosecutor who never lost a case. None of us now was what each claimed to have been then. It could have been a commercial, with some unknown has-been gaining more fame than he ever could have lost by plugging a product that had no relation to his original claim to fame. Not quite, where have you gone, Joe DiMaggio, but still...

When the bartender didn't speak up, Miriam asked what he had done or been.

"You wouldn't think to look at me, but I was an astronaut," he said, although he looked no different from any of the sons of ex-astronauts or the pictures of ex-astronauts I ever saw.

But anyone could claim to be anyone here, and not

to challenge anyone was to admit you were lying. When nobody asked, he went on to tell about the conditioning program, where they push your eyeballs to see if you can take the G-force of re-entry, and then lock you in a chamber in a space suit to teach you how to shit and eat. The missions he had been on were shuttle flights nobody would remember. It was all a little too detailed to be convincing, like a junior high scientist spewing all he had learned to anyone who couldn't get away.

One by one, people left, some not finishing drinks. Even when we were the only customers, Miriam didn't show him up by pulling it out.

"That's what I like about these suckers — you don't need to flash 'em, just wearing 'em is enough," she said when we were outside.

The streets flashed neon Christmas, dotting a line between bars, and I remembered how I had draped the medal around her neck our last day in Seattle, when we hadn't been so open to each other.

"Miriam, you know how I said it wasn't a gift? It wasn't but it is."

She stopped to hold me and didn't say a word. Jukebox tunes and fog horns dueled in the distances as we stood outside a shop lit with burglar lights to protect its invaluable antique maps of the delta in gold frames, brass parts from riverboat wheelhouses, spyglasses, ashtrays commemorating the British getting slaughtered in that meaningless battle after the end of the War of 1812, and other relics gussied up in the gloss of eternal chintz. This could have been where we bought our house gift, because it was just as remarkably unremarkable as that place had been.

"Don't you pity the wealthy?" I had said on that day we arrived, meaning their attics must be inversions of these window displays. When she said nothing, I

thought she was only angry about shopping because neither of us liked to shop, because a legit house guest
would have brought something from elsewhere instead
of a last minute trinket. The idea of having to splurge on
souvenir trash made her want to skip the visit, and as
we went from shop to shop, she got more and more
upset, until I finally got the picture that it wasn't the
idea of any piece-of-trash house gift or the prospect of a
visit to people she didn't know or anything remotely
like those things that gave her the creeps.

It didn't matter what we bought, I kept reminding
her. We could look for something unusual, since who
knew what they liked?

"I would say it's the thought that counts, if our main
thought wasn't to sneak into snazzy digs," didn't raise a
squawk. She wouldn't say what was eating her, so
rather than pick some bland nicety, I went for broke.
Not the jockey: the Mannequin Pis.

She didn't laugh.

Neither did Artie, when I handed it over. After giving our host a Mannequin Pis, we deserved any disgrace
he could devise. There was an endless pause, and then
Susan said she couldn't think of a better gift. But a five-
foot cherub with a two-inch dick trussed up in a red
bow was more than the kids could stand, and once they
started, we couldn't stop laughing, except for Miriam,
who cried.

In our room she told me, on the condition I not tell
them.

"We can't tell them nothing."

"I don't care."

"What if we say that twenty years ago your
boyfriend was killed by a mugger on Charles Street and
you don't want to talk about it? That's not so bad. I
mean, it's horrible, it's like the end of the world, but it

isn't, it's — "

"Sure, why not? You used to do that kind of work, didn't you? Nothing but a little positive spin, neat and tidy."

"Go ahead, unload on me. Make me feel rotten that I brought you here, and while you're at it, tell me how retracing your way through this does no good. So he wasn't just a boyfriend, but your first love. Your last love, since love could never be the same. You were going to start a new life with him, but then some junkie with a gun had other plans, so maybe you flinched and he freaked, maybe you were doing what the gunman said but you flinched and made him think he had to shoot, or maybe nobody had any time to think or worst of all, there was no reason."

She stopped crying and said, "One moment you are the way you are, and then you're not. You're dripping with blood and bits of skull and brain and the one you love is nothing but a writhing blob, all in a flash that's over, and over, and over, and over.

"I tell you, though, I knew right then that this was the worst, that it would never again be as bad as this, this dead hand grabbing with one last gush and everything stops but the sirens."

0

I wasn't born in Florida, but it felt like my first home. Before moving there, we went to Miami every year to visit my grandmother, so my earliest memories came from those two-week stints in the middle of winter where the weather wasn't miserable and you could swim every day.

"I don't care what anyone says about cancer, I'm gonna get a tan," she dug out her shades hours before dawn, ready for action in the Sunshine State. "I used to tan like a champ, and you had to be nothing but a bronze god, golden boy."

"King and Queen of the Wet Dream Prom," I said, "we'll hit the beach and show no mercy."

Travel wasn't going to be easy the last week of the year. Jacksonville, Miami, and towns in between cranked up festivals and parades, jacking prices here as in New Orleans, whether there was a football game in the bargain or not. Some counties had nearly made sleeping in your car a capital crime, so there was no way to beat them by crashing on the beach. In Florida you could get arrested for bad breath, yet for all the backs we destroyed, Gold Medal Health Spas paid almost no fines in my adopted home state, where for years after 1972, a well-placed campaign appearance paid my dues as a favorite son. The trick was, not to buck the system. You didn't have to go to Disneyworld — just look like they would let you in.

Stopping for gas in Pensacola, I took stock as I might if we were an outgunned army counting bullets before the last hopeless charge. We had no tans and our clothes were black and blue. Although we were old enough, we had no kids. How was it we could drive around endlessly? The land of the retired wasn't going to like what we had to say. If we weren't bad enough, there was the car.

In each hand I held a cup of awful coffee, in my mouth a bag of doughnuts as Miriam pounded an unidentified insect so that dust off the dashboard formed a noxious cloud. We never washed the car. That had been Boyd's job, and with Boyd long dead, Miriam said that it wouldn't have been right to keep it clean. Other than an oil change, she had nothing done. On the highway, nobody cared how your car looked. In town, though, a stranger couldn't hang out in a heap, and Florida had no cities big enough to make our junker disappear.

Then there was the noise it made, more like a Harley than a Chevy, but no self-respecting biker would have put up with the misfires. Not only that, it smoked. A daily can of 50-weight couldn't keep it from spewing. The car was all that remained of Boyd's estate, that rental empire he had kept tabs on from this sofa of a front seat, even though his buildings were so close together that he shouldn't have missed the chance to exercise. When the car finally did blow up, we could walk away clean, and so for no other reason, it was something I'd miss.

"You haven't thought about what we're going to do,

other than get a tan?" I said.

"What does anyone do and why not keep doing it?"

"We're running out of road and the car won't last much longer."

"That's a solution, not a problem."

"Florida's no desert island. It'll take more than coconuts to keep us going, or weren't you planning on going anywhere else?"

"Planning schmanning, aren't you the worrywart! Get this," she unfurled a roll and riffled it under my nose, "we're still holding. Reno and Riparian took care of business and left us with nothing but bills to play."

Why not let it ride?

"Sorry, I don't know what got into me."

I started the car and snapped on the radio to another song we'd heard a million times from the never neverland childhood of a collective past, where the daughters were raised by dog-handicapping uncles because their mothers couldn't be bothered, and the sons were raised by swimming coaches because their parents wanted them to become champions. We drove out of our clouds and back onto the interstate, to glide over the swamps at 60 miles an hour toward an unlikely collision with the sun.

Miriam didn't want to go to Jacksonville. Nobody would be in that trailer park by the river now. She was fourteen when they moved in with her mother's brother, old enough to know they hadn't left Jersey to find a better life but because they had run out of money.

Miriam and her Uncle Willie couldn't stand the guys her mother picked up. Cracker, Swamp Rat, Gomer, Deadhead, Gyrene, and Lounge Act came in no particular order. At least she didn't bring them to the trailer, and it got so she didn't call when staying out overnight.

"She had to make up for all the fun she never had," said Miriam, without making it sound like a pathetic grope or a romantic quest.

We were exhausted and could barely fight the glare cutting through the trees, even though we had made the turn past Tallahassee and were no longer headed due east.

"You wouldn't have done the same?"

"It wasn't what she did, but what she said. Once she said it, she couldn't take it back: 'I shoulda had the abortion.'"

We pulled over at an informal rest area, where it was okay to piss on your tires. Carloads of college kids were beginning to stir, and when they left, they left no beer cans, puke, or fast food wrappers. Between us and a lake was a stretch of high grass, with no path to the water. A couple of palms, some cypress, and enough moss to fill in the edges of the scene made it a picture I remembered right out of Swannie River, but then ever since Miriam had spotted the real Suwannee on the map leading to Fosterville, we couldn't get the song out of our heads. From lily pads to hidden flowers, water to grass to birds and certain reptiles, this place gave the warning of look-but-don't-touch.

It was dark when we awoke, but not from the night. Somehow the thunder missed us, and what hadn't been more than a dreamy hiss turned out to be a downpour. The windows were blurs, the roof a rattle as smells from the upholstery and our clothes dangled a sweet fart until we realized it wasn't from us but from the sulfury smell of the muck.

I didn't want to drive through this, and we were afraid to stay. Water filled the lot up to where our hubcaps would have been, so we might not have been able to roll. We didn't know the time or how far we were from anyplace, and although we should have been hungry, we were disoriented. It felt too cold, but the sudden clearing was no surprise, until the hard light set off everything in a steamy glimmer.

With water everywhere, you didn't want to walk around barefoot, and Miriam wasn't about to ruin her sneakers. She swung out over the excess lake after having me check for alligators, and when she finished pissing she had to hang out for a while, not wanting to swing back until I saw what she saw.

The car gleamed like never before. Parked in water, surrounded by dinosaur plants, it looked too good not to sell. Not only the car, but every corner of this backwater rest area had been transformed by the flood into my childhood couch painting, an art-by-checklist kind of picture meeting all of the minimum requirements of swamp beauty.

"Let's get out of here before it changes back," I said, hoping there was enough gravel under us so we wouldn't spin.

There was, but we couldn't blast off and risk bottoming out. More boat than car, we watched our wake as we gurgled onward, and when we made the pavement, I kept pumping to make sure the brakes weren't full of fish.

"Forget about stopping — why can't we go?"

"Maybe it's nothing," I said, but ten miles later we still couldn't make 40.

If it had been an airplane instead of a boat, we couldn't wait another moment to strap on the parachutes. This stretch of Alternate 27 had two lanes going each way, so we could poke along without causing a wreck. If we met a tractor or a narrow bridge, a shoulder wasn't going to save us.

"What's the next town?" I said, as if I hadn't known.

Fosterville wasn't just a dot on the map, and it was more than a pit stop. Most people knew it for the infamous river and the wax museum advertised on hundreds of billboards, but my path had crossed Fosterville's because of something else.

It wasn't a question of health spas. The nearest branch had been down the coast, in a part of Tampa nobody confused with St. Petersburg.

"Chick, no!"

"Florida's own Ken Honochick," said the next wax museum billboard, in a reasonably accurate likeness, even if the medals were unmistakably large.

"You know me, I don't like to spoil surprises."

Fosterville, December, 1972: Jill and I hadn't been in the room a minute before the argument resumed. As Grand Marshals of the first annual Gold Bowl, we rated better than a motel with walls that didn't stop the slightest noise. I calmed her by telling about an old swimming coach, someone who pushed what Roger Patterson would later refer to as the gym teacher-induced inhibitions that thwart self-actualization, and once she understood that the guys in the other room meant none of what they said, except as a prod to get us to do what they wanted, she also thought it was funny.

I used to claim that the phony abuse that was calculated to build mental toughness never bothered me, but there had been a sour moment in the Games. I was to compete in the medley relay, but didn't. An easy third gold medal I passed up (practically handed to) a teammate who hadn't yet won one. I should have been thanked and praised, but there was an unspoken notion that I had dogged it. Swim through the pain, they always said, yet to swim with the cramps I had would have blown a chance for any medal, even if a few didn't see it that way. Then we won, my doubters forgot, and the next day when the shooting started, nobody cared about a swimmer with a limp.

"He can't be that bad. Nobody's that bad."

"Roger, even if we dub the voice, the video doesn't lie."

"Perception, Rick, perception, and Peter my man, Peter, what we have here is not a hopeless case, but a challenge! Gentlemen, need I remind you, although it shouldn't be necessary, one word."

"Not again."

"Don't pretend it didn't happen."

"It's not anywhere near — "

"One word, not perception, not stiff or dub or even challenge, one word: Nixon."

"Roger, it's not anywhere near the same. Face it, it's not my daughter he ran off with."

"He did not run off with."

"Whatever, marry, so they're married, and you've got a son-in-law with a couple of gold medals and we're happy for you and they can't take that away, but Roger, this is business. They bought Nixon because he had no competition. They are not going to buy Honochick because what they really want is Spitz. So all right, say we send him to acting school and make him a video Romeo, now you pretend he isn't your son-in-law, and tell me, why?"

They wouldn't keep it down. It was no secret my screen test had been a flop. This running debate around the agency on whether to dump the spas and eat my contract wasn't new, yet they yammered away constantly from New York to Fosterville. They punished us for not caring about their problems, and we cared even less. We laughed at them, but they couldn't get rid of me until they tried one more test.

"Gentlemen," said Roger, not loudly, for once, "it's out of our hands: let the people decide."

No amount of training or editing had made me the charmer they wanted, but Gold Medal Health Spas wasn't shooting for prime time slickness. At the end of 1972, Roger Patterson was ready to bet on the counterculture, by which he meant not the anti-war movement but cut-rate production values and spots on late night TV. Rick and Peter were underlings and, unlike most bosses, he encouraged them to oppose him. This hid his true position, so when asked by the investors why suchand-such didn't fly, he could shed responsibility.

"Let the people decide," was his line of the week, rephrased from "Power to the People" so nobody would take him for a radical. In terms of my tie to the agency, it meant they would give me one last chance before scrapping the spas, annulling the marriage, and cutting their losses. Since the promo campaign came down to whistle-stop appearances and Veg-o-matic style commercials, nothing mattered beyond connecting "on a personal level with the people."

I never found out what that meant. At the time, the worst case (getting paid $100,000 to scram) didn't seem so bad. Jill and I even thought we'd have fun sneaking around after the annulment. There was no pressure to succeed. And then, my success was unqualified. The people decided I could do no wrong, and in the end the skeptics agreed the project should go on.

They were mistaken. So intent they were on finding a hostile environment for a foolproof test, they didn't see that Fosterville, Florida, was the worst possible proving ground. Fosterville was a town on the make, in

1972 as now, no matter when now was. In the heart of nowhere, it felt like a border town. Stephen Foster had never been there, but after his big hit they renamed the place to go with the river. The first roadside stands sold fruit and more later added snake farms, monkey jungles, and unfiltered aquarium pastures for sea cows. Nothing ever failed, it re-organized. In the mid-1950s, the wax museum got listed as a map attraction, and its collection of the famous and infamous evolved from World Famous to World Class. Paddle wheelers and military landing craft gave rides eighteen hours a day, and, unchecked by city planning, sections of town variously changed themselves into Bavarian Villages, Frontier Trading Posts, and Mystic Seaports. An illegal Seminole reservation made it legal for them to sell heavy duty fireworks. Nobody minded. People needed a place to buy contraband they couldn't buy anywhere else. If I couldn't make it there, I couldn't make it anywhere.

The hustlers of Fosterville weren't satisfied with the fruit stands and boat rides, the fireworks armory, wax museum, snake farm, World's Fair architecture, and pacesetting sales of cute bumper stickers. In Florida they reckoned you had to have a bowl game, and with syndicated networks snapping the rights to anything involving college football that happened in December, the hustlers announced (never stopping to realize they had no place to play) in early 1972 that Fosterville, Florida, would on December 30th of that year host the first annual Olympic Bowl.

The International Olympic Committee made a phone call, and the next day they announced the name wouldn't be Olympic, but Gold: the Gold Bowl.

The hustlers were masters of making the best of a negative turn of events. The tragedy of the Munich Olympics was just a brief setback for this town without pity. Their answers to criticism that they were exploiting a disaster were a slogan, "Celebrate the Good," and thousands of lapel buttons of upthrust thumbs that didn't mean, "stick it up your ass."

Years later, Roger Patterson confessed that the agency had cut a deal with Fosterville way before the Olympics, and, like the town hustlers, the agency wasn't about to let a massacre change its plans. Spitz had been everyone's first choice, even though many worried that his being Jewish wouldn't let people forget what had happened. When Spitz was unavailable, the agency was relieved to get me, not so much because of my medals but because of my non-Jewish background. I had strict orders to downplay "the Jewish thing," and the three of them put me through fake interrogations to make sure I wouldn't say something insensitive.

Never mind that the hustlers of Fosterville made sure that their precious Gold Bowl got only friendly press coverage, that I would field no question more provocative than, "How do you feel about changing the anthem to 'America the Beautiful'?"

The fake interrogations backfired, not making me dread the real press conference, but setting me up to enjoy it. I performed better than I would have ordinarily, so it seemed I couldn't miss as a figurehead spokesman.

There we were in our costumes in the middle of the room while Rick and Peter walked around smoking and yelling questions and Roger Patterson watched, and since our costumes were bathing suits, the flunkies didn't spare us their stares.

"Where were you on the night of the massacre and when did you get the idea things weren't as they should have been?"

"We heard the shots, but you don't think of them as shots until someone tells you."

"Was there nothing you could do to help? Wasn't there talk of some sort of swap, a Mark-Spitz-for-all-the-Israeli-hostages kind of deal?"

"I don't believe a single member of the American Olympic Team wouldn't have willingly traded places with the hostages."

"What are your feelings about the Palestine issue — not you, this is for the girl."

"I — I don't believe we have enough information to make an informed decision."

"So you don't think the news is unbiased?"

"I didn't say that."

"Considering the circumstances, don't the Palestinians have a right to go to extremes? Suppose positions were reversed, and the PLO had a home but the Jews did not. Wouldn't the Jews be justified in taking the Palestine athletes hostage, even murdering them one by one until their demands were met?"

"Murder is never justifiable," I said.

"Suppose I were to tell you that this isn't murder, but an act of war? Surely you can't expect a third-world gang of ad hoc freedom fighters to be able to fight a modern army on first world/apple pie/Geneva Convention terms?"

"The Olympic Games is not about war, it's about peace. Thank you, gentlemen, for your questions, but I'm afraid we can't solve the world's problems here and now; besides, we have a parade to lead."

"Cut, excellent," said Roger Patterson, "didn't I tell you?"

"I don't know, let's try it one more time."

"Jill darling, Ken my son, it's up to nobody but you. If you feel absolutely confident, if you can say with complete authority that nothing can go wrong, then we'll call it a night."

I gave him the thumbs up that didn't mean, "A-O.K."

"Jill, Jill honey, you're not shivering, you're not afraid, are you?"

"No, Daddy, I'm freezing. Cut the crap and give me a blanket," she uncorked a sneeze.

"Didn't I tell you: they're naturals."

Miriam and I didn't have to contend with the bowl game. With the interstate highway replacing Alternate 27 and Route 19 as the way south from Atlanta, Fosterville had fallen into the timelessness of the roadside past. Events like the Gold Bowl came and went, and somehow the town made the conversion from a place people went through to a place people went to, for low-rent vacations and no-frills honeymoons.

Blushing couples were everywhere, necks full of hickeys and eyes glazed with sleepless lust. You could hear them from the street, the cafes, and the riverside, since the next motel room was never far away.

"When in Rome," said Miriam, snuggling up to me in our booth at the Zephyr House while we waited for word on the car, but we didn't look like honeymooners.

"What's the age of consent around here, twelve?" she said, and when I didn't say, "or maybe they wink if you're in uniform."

After lunch we strolled through Bavaria via the Monkey Jungle among the soldiers, sailors, and storm troopers with their child brides, but it was impossible to avoid the museum any longer.

"Wait, you can't charge us. Don't you know this guy's an inmate, a model, a star?"

The cashier not much older than a bride squinted.

"Chick, take it off, then she won't play dumb."

"No thanks, I'd rather pay."

"Oh no you don't. They can't put Ken Honochick on a billboard without letting him in free."

An older woman came out of nowhere.

"Mr. Honochick, you don't know how honored we are!"

"Aw, it's noth— "

"Don't pay attention to him, just lead the way and let him go one-on-one with Mr. Candlehead."

"Actually, uh, Mrs. Honochick, Ken here has never failed to draw a crowd."

"I don't doubt it."

The museum wasn't crowded, yet an audience filled in behind us, giving space to see the figures from history, culture, and crime, in settings that told you who they were, if the likenesses didn't. The unknowns made famous by bloodshed were more popular than the others, yet most of the attractions added recently weren't from life: they were from the movies.

"In fact," the guide added, "the McCulloch Company was generous to design these super-lightweight chainsaw replicas specifically for the Fosterville Wax Museum," indirectly pointing out what all the movies had in common.

The sports section was mostly football, but out of respect for authenticity, the wax museum couldn't arm the players. For baseball, there were beanings and thrown bats, and a special display of the collision between my Reno crony Spike and his teammate Ewell the Mule that made no bones about showing the compound fracture. After this, "Deaths in the Ring" seemed tame, even when it went from boxing to bull fighting, but when asked why there were no scenes from dog racing, our guide said people were touchy about dogs.

"And now, brace yourselves," said the guide, "the Fosterville Wax Museum presents its masterpiece, and not only that, the man behind the wax, in the flesh!" She turned down the lights and on came a tape of a generic college fight song as a curtain parted to reveal the background of screams and gunfire, and a banner unfurled in the foreground: "Victory at Munich."

"He thought his work was done when he took the gold in the 100-meter and the 200-meter backstroke, but then an army of terrorists raided the Olympic Village, and Ken Honochick of Miami, Florida, had another job to do," went a voice that wouldn't have had it any other way.

There I was in my tank suit, belt of ammo over one shoulder, buxom gymnast in a ripped leotard around one leg, while a platform swiveled so my Uzi mowed down Yasser Arafat look-alikes without so much as nicking the hostages they used for shields.

"Nothing tops celebrating the good," I said.

"No fooling," said Miriam, "but who's the tootsie?"

The voice said, "Outgunned but not outmanned, the American champion took back the night, not to take part, but to win; not for the struggle, but for the triumph; not just to fight well, but to conquer."

The lights went up, the curtain closed, and none of them didn't cheer. They were eager to see the movie, and it did no good to tell them it hadn't been made, let alone to say the exhibit was based on the worst kind of lie. Many of them wanted my autograph, not for what I had done, but for what the wax museum had me do. I didn't doubt that these grooms would have deserted their brides for a shot at taking my place on the world stage of revenge.

"It wasn't like that! I didn't do anything but swim a few heats. I never saw her before. I don't even know how to use a — "

"Modesty will get you nowhere," said Miriam.

I refused to spend another moment in this tartar sauce town where the gas of fried fish never cleared. We didn't wait for them to rebuild the engine, and traded blind for an older Chevy that got worse mileage, had balder tires, and would probably cost more to repair than the other one. I didn't care, as long as it could cruise the fast lane.

"Lighten up, Chick, everything isn't a wax museum."

I couldn't answer. It was too late for me to get high and mighty about ethics, and to say they used me against my will wouldn't have been exactly correct. True, I knew nothing about the diorama remake, but hadn't my skid down promo lane been a spinout of sellouts? After winning over Fosterville in December, 1972, I had no excuse not to cooperate. I liked getting stroked — who wouldn't? It wasn't easy keeping cool and neutral as a beauty queen. It was a challenge, and for a while, I could pretend I was a diplomat, sacrificing a little to gain a lot, and not only for me but for all concerned. It wasn't small potatoes to be a model for a national fitness company. Too many people depended on me for me to go shooting my mouth off about Vietnam, the PLO, and all that, and my opinions were barely notions, deformed by careless glances at headlines and the evening news. You could say I was like most people, but most people didn't get paid big bucks to smile. Most people didn't outswim the world going backwards, only to wind up as wax idols, beer commercial rejects, phantom owners of racing greyhounds, and garbage sifters whose claim to fame stumped the trivia wizards of a nostalgia show.

We left town the only way I knew, by none other than the parade route.

"It couldn't have been colder, but we were troupers. We stood and waved and tried not to get out of the sun-lamps they rigged around the convertible. As an ex-Rose Queen, Jill was a big hit, and being her escort didn't hurt my image."

Miriam and I came to the Gold Bowl, which hadn't been relabeled after the game fell through, at least a decade ago. The 30,000 temporary extra bleachers still stood, closing in the ends to make it look like a college stadium and not just a high school field.

"You know, sometimes these meaningless match-ups of also-rans put on the best shows. I don't remember who won, but the score was 49-48. They had me lip-synch the national anthem from an Olympic winners' stand, then dragged us out at halftime for a song and dance, and at the end of the game, we gave out trophies, riding the coattails of a wild game nobody was supposed to care about. Years later, I was still getting asked to be on sports call-in shows to talk about that game, and they didn't even sugarcoat it by saying we'd also talk about me."

As advertised, the beater made 60 without a whine. In the rearview I read the billboards for the wax muse-um, and once more found myself over Alternate 27, in that pose uncluttered by bullets and guns.

The older new car looked better than the newer old one, but we didn't take long to change that. We filled it with throwaway souvenirs: local beer and supermarket Key lime pie, which didn't look as bad as they tasted. We went to the laundromat and cleaned up to fit in, to become part of Florida and not just some parasite the body would reject.

Dog racing was all around, and there were other temptations, but we were undistracted. The farther south we went, the whiter the land got and the bluer the sky, and as the smells became familiar, I talked less and Miriam didn't interrupt. We'd switched coasts and followed Route 1 when we couldn't take A-1-A.

"You know, Chick, I never lived on the beach, but at least that trailer park was on the water. Whaddya say we pick a spot on a river, or if not there, on a bay or canal?"

"If the barracuda don't get you, the nettles will, and that's not counting the snakes."

"On it, not in it."

I knew what she meant, and I also knew it wasn't true what they said about alligators always keeping to themselves.

As we got out of the land of the open road and into the land of home, with schools and stores, libraries and community swimming pools, Miriam wanted to know if they'd named a pool after me, but I wasn't the only Olympian from here, and pools were named after the people who donated the money to build them.

We went by the old high school, the burger joints and teenage dance halls that had been turned into other burger joints and warehouses, the grocers who now sold fresh squeezed juice where there used to be one of a chain of convenience stores that went out of business, the ex-houses of girls I had wanted for girlfriends, and nothing I remembered made any of these places special.

What stood out instead were places I went with my parents as we visited their friends, people over fifty when I was under ten, men whose legs had been shot off in Europe and women who wore wigs because they had no hair, men with arthritis who took me fishing and women with cancer who gave me chicks for Easter. There had been one woman who went skin diving with me, who married a rich guy twice her age, but when I counted the years, I saw no way she would still be alive, either.

I hadn't been back since my grandmother died. Not that I would have gone to reunions.

We had moved so much, my mother and father didn't get buried in the same cemetery, even though they died just a state and a few months apart. Our house in North Miami was typical, in that it was indistinguishable from the one next door. Both were sided with crushed white stone, to match the driveways, and both were surrounded by the tropical grass that's thicker and darker than regular grass and seems to grow not upward but sideways, like a ground-hugging beanstalk. We had been the only family along the canal without a boat.

"Not bad, Chick. How'd you blow the inheritance, or didn't they own what they could rent?"

"It came at a bad time, when I didn't need it but had lawyers to pay."

"Why not introduce ourselves and snoop around. They won't mind."

"Not much. Every other stranger in Miami these days packs more heat than a police force because each of them thinks every other stranger packs more dope than a mule team, and you want to tell them not to worry, that we're not here to sell them encyclopedias."

"There's nothing wrong with the truth. I used to live here and I won't be a bother if you'd please let me look around. All they can say is yes or no."

"No. I used to live here, then I didn't, then I kicked butt in the Olympics, and if you let me, I'll prove it in your pool."

"Chi-ick, don't be grumpy."

"I'm not interested."

"Don't I have some say? Suppose I want to look?" but she saw I didn't want to, although I was beginning to think I did.

Radio had been taken over by all-time hit countdowns, so you would go from the Fab Five Hundred to the Hot Hundred to the Top Ten as the end of the year approached, but here we could listen to Cuban stations, not caring that the completely unfamiliar also ran together and sounded the same.

We found a vacancy in a waterfront motel that had no beach left to cover a rusted bulkhead and a drain pipe, which saved us the trouble of stepping in tar and Portuguese Man-O-Wars, fish hooks, and other hazards that made a walk in the sand no picnic. Not that we had time for fun in the sun. We spent New Year's Eve Day going through thrift stores in this place where the well-heeled come to die, and we found what we wanted in the right size, without having to settle for less.

White tie would have been too dressy, and black tie was fine as long as the tie was red, but Miriam bought a gown that was better than red, whether or not she felt like stopping traffic.

We found a snazzy restaurant that didn't make you spring for a New Year's Eve package, where most of the customers didn't look young enough to last past midnight. Very slowly, and with a wine that cost as much as a night in a better-than-average motel, we ate cold stone crab dipped in hot butter: not just a meal, but an object lesson in how to live. The dining room was one of those art deco palaces, with pillars and chandeliers, a fountain

courtyard dance floor and a stage for a big band that
would never be as big as it once had been. It was a place
that had often celebrated but these days couldn't help
but regret recognizing the passing of another year.

We doubled back to cross the bay on the antique
Venetian Causeway rather than take the more conven-
ient route, and as we turned up Biscayne Boulevard, I
wondered whether we shouldn't have stayed in the
restaurant. That would have been okay with Miriam,
who hadn't expected this extension of our night on the
town. The meal had been perfect, and, depressing or
not, you couldn't beat the ambience. Why not quit early,
pick up a bottle, and make the most of our bed by the
sea?

"We're going to a party!" she squealed, not listening
to all I had said, probably because it was so rare for me
to stage an elaborate date on New Year's Eve.

"No," I tried, but the distinction was lost. "We are
not going to a party. We go to the door, we knock and
we say we're looking for a party at the Hendersons, and
when they say the Hendersons don't live here, we get
our peek."

"These duds ought to be worth a full-blown gander,
and I don't care who knows it. How about, I break a
strap and ask for a safety pin, offer no less than an eye-
ful for a peek?"

Had I really thought Miriam wouldn't change
things? Maybe unconsciously, that's what I really wanted, to use her as a battering ram to get into the house of
my earliest memories, where my grandmother lived
when going to Florida meant coming home.

Thank you notes must have made the address
indelible, but I didn't need a number or directions. I
turned off the main drag to that residential parkway,
with its lanes separated by a row of coconut trees, in a

neighborhood that wasn't much different from all I remembered, right down to the yellow glow of the porch lights, the stucco walls, the red tile roofs. And there was the brick patio entrance past an unlocked gate, to the door knocker with the head of a dragon.

Could it be the yard hadn't changed? Around here, you didn't let plants go wild or they'd take over, but the new people hadn't cut back the overgrowth protecting the rock where the chameleons from the circus lived.

Miriam gripped my arm, giggling, and there was nothing to do but follow as she pushed in without knocking, bellowing hello.

My pail was a paint can, my paint water, and I couldn't let up before it dried. I did every brick on the wall and down the patio, not painting myself into a corner. The dull brown turned shiny red and made me want to do the door, even if the colors weren't the same.

My toys were tools, and I played work, never finding enough to do. I got up at dawn, and moved the chairs into the yard, and buried the cards that were diamonds, and when they made me put it all back, I didn't mind.

We were on vacation, so they slept late and I got up early, and then one morning I fixed my grandmother Lucille's Buick because the holes in the side didn't go through. Their tools were my toys, but they didn't work better than my plastic ones, except to wake everyone up and make them angry.

They sent me to my room, away from my chores, not letting me out to eat. They told me to think about how bad I had been, and they wouldn't say when I could leave.

Finally, they came for me with a new idea, and made me put on my bathing suit, but we didn't go to the ocean. We went to a place where the water was bluer than ocean blue and very clear, inside walls with checkers of light and dark blue around the top that stayed still until someone walked the plank and bounced to fly into a splash that unstoppered funny smells.

My mother said I wasn't allowed to pee because this wasn't the ocean. In the ocean they pulled or carried me, but now that I was old enough to swim, it was better if she didn't teach me.

She gave me to a girl with rubber hair, who told me her name and not to be afraid. She took me by the hand, and we went down the steps one at a time, stopping at each so I could feel the water coming up, and she told me she wouldn't let go until I was ready, because the water would soon be over my head. She gleamed as she dunked, and when it was my turn, I didn't see why she was so pleased, why each dunk, kick, or splash I did made her say what a good, brave boy I was.

I liked coming to the pool, but I learned not to believe her. When she wasn't saying how great I was, she was backing away. We'd start a few feet apart and no matter how hard I swam, she would be the same distance away, waving for me to keep coming. She kept her arms out, trusting me no more than I trusted her.

My reward was lunch at the cafeteria, where you got dessert first and soup last, such a good idea that they had to tell me not to eat until we got through the line. Or Lucille would buy me what my parents wouldn't let me have, Pepsi Cola, because it took the paint off cars. We didn't talk about the Buick, and everything was fixed because I was learning to swim.

I don't remember when they said the land was one big river flowing down through the Everglades and that the canal behind Lucille's house had alligators, but it couldn't have yet been 1959 when I stood on the brink of water and knew that everything was possible.

"Time to go home," someone said, although the sun wouldn't be up for hours.

Nobody stayed up all night any more. These people were no younger than we were, but they had begun to leave right after midnight. If they didn't have babysitters to relieve, they had to rest so they could watch football. Some were even going to the Orange Bowl, and when we were offered tickets, we had to make up an excuse so it didn't look weird that we didn't want them.

Eugene the host didn't care if we stayed, and Gayle the hostess hit it off with Miriam like a long lost pal. It didn't hurt that Miriam begged him to keep playing the baby grand.

The piano hadn't belonged to Lucille as much as to the house. They bought both a couple of years ago from a name I didn't know, and when he bragged about how little he paid, I hoped Miriam wasn't getting too cozy with them.

Most of these people seemed to know each other, but nobody asked why we were here. They weren't dressed up as we were, but all were more or less polished. You didn't have to ask what anyone did. When people introduced themselves and shook hands, we didn't lie, we said we were freelance.

I couldn't blame them for having interesting careers that kept them in style. These lawyers, accountants, salesmen, doctors, and mid-level media executives could stand in line when society passed out the good conduct medals, and that wasn't counting the fact that most of them had kids. Even more than Artie Gifford, they were driven to succeed, and, looking around my grandmother's house, I couldn't complain that it had fallen into their hands. The furniture was even similar, with the oriental rug over most of the off-white coral floor, the world in a sofa, and the chairs of irresistible cushions. Unlike the piano, these weren't exactly what I remembered, but one other thing had made it through the changes of owners, the "Swannie River" painting. Sure, it was only a couch painting, but I thought more of them for not taking it down.

Miriam had hit the ground running and not looked back, greeting one and all. Instead of watching her operate, I made my way, nodding and trying not to get lost in the fixtures, molding, and patterns that were all so disturbing in an impersonal yet intimate way. She kept an eye on me, too, and winked to let me know she wouldn't give me away.

I also did my part of chatting them up, so I wouldn't seem like a total mooch, and it amazed me how much we got out of that restaurant in Miami Beach, which they recognized and hadn't yet visited, even though it was "right up there on the list." Nobody went out as much as they wanted, especially since nobody was from here and wanted to see more of the area. Many of them, too, remembered this place as a paradise from vacations taken long ago, and none now regretted coming here to live. We all talked about the Golden Age, when people drank not wine but liquor, and ate not sashimi but pigs in blankets.

On trips to the bathroom, I saw that almost nothing had been renovated. This wasn't just a New Year's Eve theme party. Every nook looked thirty years older, from the fiestaware plates and lobster claw salt-and-pepper shakers in the dining room to the dated *Life*s sprawled over end tables, so that it wasn't a home so much as a museum.

I didn't ask my way. Getting lost was license to roam, in case somebody found me where I wasn't supposed to be. The bedrooms went around a courtyard, hacienda style, so I couldn't turn on lights without letting people see me from the party rooms, but then there was just one spot I wanted, and what light there was would do.

The kid seemed unreal. I didn't know how long he'd been here, but then he said, "Tell me a story," not startled or scared.

"You don't want to hear any of my stories. My stories have no morals, they go the wrong way, and the heroes aren't people you'd want to be or even meet. Don't you want a drink of water, instead?"

"I'm not thirsty."

"Why don't you tell me a story?"

"Once upon a time there was a deer, named Bambi," he said, and by the way he looked at me, I knew he wasn't fooling around.

"Christ, kid, not that!"

He wouldn't listen; his eyes got bigger and his voice lowered into a song of a sob.

"Bambi's mother loved Bambi, and they lived happily in the forest, until the hunters came," he couldn't hold back the tears, "and killed Bambi's mother, and made Bambi an orphan and burned down the forest and made Bambi sad ever after."

"Don't take it so hard, kid. That's nothing but lies. Life gets better," I said, whether he believed me or not.

Back in the living room, Miriam sang while Eugene played and more people got ready to leave, some tooting noisemakers to beat the band while others just tried not to smash things on their way out.

"Amateur Night," said Miriam, "people don't know how to drink any more. Hey Gayle, what say we steal their car keys so they don't kill anyone?"

"They're not going anywhere," said Eugene. "They live here, don't you?"

"I live wherever I am," said Miriam, before her next request: "Nothing Could Be Finer."

She pulled me to her, and as we danced, I thought of the road they had taken and the road that we had taken, of their house here and of our car outside, and I knew that nothing could.

Doug Nufer writes novels, poems, and plays that can appear to follow various odd procedures, even when they don't. His novels *Negativeland, Never Again,* and *On the Roast* and his CD *The Office* were not originally intended to be released by different publishers in the same year.

More Unbearable Books
for your edification and amusement

The Unbearables' Unbearables

An anthology of fictive adventures by the Unbearables and collaborators, a free-floating in-your-face scrum of black humorists, chaos-mongers, immediatists, and verse-spouting Beer Mystics©, disorganized around recuperating essence away from the humorless commodification of experience. Includes: Judy Nylon, Max Blagg, Bikini Girl, Bruce Benderson, Hakim Bey, Jordan Zinovich, and the Unbearables.

1-57027-053-8   288 pp. 6" x 9" $14

Crimes of the Beats

One evening, the Unbearable Beatniks of Light were bemoaning the sorry state of radical culture, and asked themselves what single act they could do to release themselves from their past, while at the same time honoring it. Perhaps put the beatniks, the real beatniks, on trial? Turn the *Crimes of the Beats* into the Nuremberg of Bohemia: Call out Burroughs for copping W. C. Fields' act, and Ginsberg for being the original Maynard G. Krebs in the gray flannel beret—always hyping, hyping, hyping the myth, then selling, selling, selling it as the only viable alternative to the polluted mainstream. And of course Jackie boy himself for claiming that he wrote *On the Road* in one sitting, a lie that ruined three whole generations of novelists gobbling speed to duplicate the feat of the beat that never really went down in anything short of seven drafts.

1-57027-069-4   224 pp. 6" x 9" $14

More Unbearable Books
for your edification and amusement

Help Yourself

In this discharge of the Unbearables' series of blasts on American culture, they dismantle, parody, and otherwise mangle the literary tradition of the Self Help Book. More than 75 individual contributors took on the topic, and in their Unbearable tradition, demolish the myths of self help in more than 75 ways. Includes work by Samuel R. Delaney, Robert Anton Wilson, Sparrow, Jim Knipfel, Arthur Nersesian, Carl Watson, Doug Nufer, Richard Kostelanetz, Tsaurah Litzky, Christian X. Hunter, Michael Carter, Jill Rapaport, Bob Holman, Ron Kolm, Susan Scutti, and more.

1-57027-104-6   192 pp. 6" x 9" $14

Wiggling Wishbone
STORIES OF PATASEXUAL SPECULATION

Bart Plantenga

A sinister collection of stories that, through force of language, reveals the limits of power and commerce. His "intelligent rage" addresses Hitler from his dog's point of view, a sexual liaison with Andy Warhol, the Pope's wet dreams, and other targets. Plantenga has been called "the William Gibson of the Lower East Side," "a punk Borges," and simply "an incredibly talented underground writer."

1-57027-009-0   160 pp. 4.5" x 7" $8

*These and many other books are available at the Autonomedia online bookstore, at **bookstore.autonomedia.org**, where you'll also find the Interactivist Info Exchange, a free-ranging and lively forum of the guiding ideas that continue to inspire the Autonomedia project.*

Spermatogonia
THE ISLE OF MAN
Bart Plantenga

A psychological snapshot of a carefully-managed identity's dissipation. In this dense novella, the narrator decides to disappear, both physically and metaphysically. At this turning point in his life, Kees Caliphora is a laughtrack technician and psychogeographer: he scouts the physical spaces and social situations that produce specific kinds of laughter, which his company then markets to the entertainment industry. His dissatisfaction is not ameliorated by fat paychecks and expense accounts, and his dubious memories of an earlier life as an art-porn star further undermine any connection with an authentic existence. Turning inward, he critically examines and casts off layer after layer of character signifiers, reaching a point of absolute interiority, a personal space between terror and spiritual calm. Ultimately discarding subjectivity itself, he finally enters a world where identity only exists as remnants of other peoples' memory. Illustrated.

1-57027-160-7   144 pp.   5.5″ x 5″ $8